A Highlander for Christmas

by

Jamie Carie

Copyright © 2013 by Jamie Carie Masopust
All rights reserved.
Printed in the United States of America

http://www.jamiecarie.com

978-0-9889097-3-1

Dewey Decimal Classification: F
Subject Heading: LOVE STORIES-FICTION

Author's Note: This novel is a work of fiction. Names, characters, places, and incidents are either products of the author's imagination or used fictitiously. All characters are fictional, and any similarity to people living or dead is purely coincidental.

All rights reserved.
No part of this publication can be reproduced or transmitted in any form or by any means, electronic or mechanical, without permission in writing from Jamie Carie Masopust.

Dedication

To my cousins, Stacey and Susie. You've shown such fortitude and grace in difficult times. May God bless you and keep you in his arms with all comfort and peace.

And to my Uncle Wayne Carie, you are greatly loved and missed.

Table of Contents

Chapter One

Chapter Two

Chapter Three

Chapter Four

Chapter Five

Chapter Six

Chapter Seven

Chapter Eight

Chapter Nine

Chapter Ten

Chapter Eleven

Epilogue

Chapter One

Glencoe, Scotland – the Year of Our Lord, 1714

The low drone of the bagpipes and rap of the drums sounded across the glen, meeting their traveling party minutes before the sights of the highland games came into view. Their large coach lumbered along the rutted road over dips and swells in the land that was becoming more mountainous and steep with every mile. The glen narrowed beneath the towering, moss-covered rock faces, giving way with each bend in the road to more of the breath-robbing beauty. It was hard to believe that each rotation of their carriage wheels brought them into further splendor, but it was true, a foreshadow of what heaven might be like.

God's waiting room.

Juliet Lindsay clung to the side of the sturdy vehicle, her face close to the window, wishing they would stop soon so that she could get out and really see the beauty surrounding them. Inside the carriage with her was her Uncle Clyde, Aunt Becca, cousin Fiona, and baby Lillian. There had been seven children born to her aunt and uncle, but only Fiona and now the new babe still breathed. Juliet shot a glance at the gurgling baby and hoped with all her heart that God's will was to see Lillian survive infancy. God's will made little sense to her—who lived and who died, who had success and who had failure, the pains of life—but she supposed she shouldn't question Him over it. Just thinking of an all-powerful, all-knowing God made her turn her thoughts quickly away in fear. It was better not to think of Him at all.

The sounds of the bagpipes grew louder and joined with the sounds of shouting and cheering. Juliet's lips turned up in excitement as they rounded another bend, and then there, lining either side of the glen, were the tents and the flags of the highland clans flapping in the wind. A hundred or more men in kilts wandered over the land, each bearing their tartans, many practicing with long poles, hammers and stones.

"Ah, lassies, 'tis a beautiful place, is it no'?" her uncle, a stout, vociferous man with wild gray hair, asked across from Juliet.

Juliet nodded, a knot in her throat preventing her from speech. Her gaze traveled like a hungry person starved for such beauty, up the sides of the moss-covered mountains, past a winsome waterfall to the rocky peaks—three of them.

"That's the three sisters, it is." Her uncle pointed toward the three mountains. "They've a mist hovering about them most the time, I suspect."

"Can we stop, please?" Fiona strained to see around Juliet.

"Only another moment, lass." Her uncle chuckled. "See that tent there? The large one with the dark red tartan a-wavin'?"

The girls nodded and Aunt Becca leaned toward her side of the window to see as well.

"That's the Clan MacLeon. Verra powerful clan, verra powerful man, Iain MacLeon. Well now, if I were a bettin' man—"

"Which you're not," Aunt Becca interjected with a frown.

Uncle Clyde cleared his throat. "That's so, that's so. But if I was, I would put me money on MacLeon. Keep an eye out for 'em, lassies. And mark my words, why—"

"They'll do well to keep away from the competitors. Och, such young and pretty girls." Aunt Becca shook her head in worriment. "I'm not sure why I let you talk me into bringing us all along."

"It's the games!" Uncle Clyde boomed. "You'll not be lettin' Miss Juliet here go home without seeing Scotland at it's best, will ya now?"

Aunt Becca cracked a smile. "I suppose not. I well remember my first games." Her eyes glassed over with the memory and a soft smile played on her lips, making Juliet wonder what she was thinking about. Aunt Becca reached over, patted Juliet's knee and winked at her, as if reading her thoughts. "'Tis hard to believe the summer is gone from us and you will be returning home soon."

Juliet nodded, her heart sinking just thinking about it. Fiona's family had a far more warm and relaxed household than her own. There had been daily horseback riding over the rolling hills no matter the weather, helping with the household chores and caring for baby Lillian, the Scottish feasts and dances that lasted far into the night and then this— the highlight of her visit, the spectacular highland games. Her time with this happy and boisterous family had gone by so quickly, had been so wonderfully refreshing, especially after her disastrous London season. She pressed her forehead against the window, seeing the breathtaking valley where they would pitch their tent, and acknowledged that she dreaded returning home.

Juliet felt her cheeks warm at the thought of the "devastation," as her mother icily referred to it, that she had caused her family. How could a grown woman of twenty full years be so foolish? Had they taught her nothing? No man would have her now, didn't she know? After the raging and shrill arguments they had packed her off to her father's older brother, chief of the small Erskine Clan, just north of Stirling Castle, for a chance to see how those not so fortunate as they lived. Her mother always referred to the highland people as barbarians, but what her mother hadn't foreseen was that Juliet would fall completely in love with her Scottish relatives and their beautiful highlands and that she would not want to ever return to Eden Place in Northumberland.

Eden Place. There was little of the Garden of Eden in the cold, windswept, barren land of her father's inheritance. As first-born son, he had inherited the English title of Earl of Wright, Baron Lindsay, with lands in northern Northumberland, but his younger brother, Clyde Lindsay, had managed to keep the chieftain title to their Scottish relations with the Clan of Erskine. Juliet wished she had been born on the Scottish side of the blanket.

"You stay together, my girls, and out of the men's

way, and all shall be well." Her aunt was continuing to speak.

Juliet nodded in agreement. After what had happened in the garden outside a ballroom in London she would be careful not to be alone with a man until she was wed, if that blessed event ever occurred.

The carriage came to a halt just beyond the MacLeon tents. Their own tents would be set up nearby, but there were no flags or tartans to mark them, as Uncle Clyde's clan wasn't participating in the games this year, only watching. He'd bemoaned the fact that he hadn't a son nor a champion worthy, but had told many a tale about the times in which they had competed during the long journey to the glen.

Juliet stepped out of the carriage and took a long, deep breath of sweet-smelling air. She took a few steps toward the edge of the road, which was little more than a two-wheeled path in the dirt, to where there was a long, grassy drop-off that led deeper into the glen. A stream meandered at the lowest point, with a field of ferns to her left as far as she could see. In front of her and farther down, the ferns gave way to moss-covered, rocky earth and then a wide, trickling stream. On the other side of the stream the rock climbed up and up toward the

Three Sisters Mountains that her uncle had pointed out in the coach. They rose into the clouds, three points of rock face coming in and out of the hovering mists. The mists moved over the tops of the three mountains with the cold breeze, giving her glimpses of their peaks.

Fiona took her hand. "Isnae it grand?"

Juliet nodded, the awe of the place making an ache in her chest. "The grandest thing I've ever seen."

"There was a terrible massacre here a few years back, can you believe? It dinnae seem possible to me."

"What happened?"

"The Clan MacDonald held land here, in Glencoe. They'd been tardy in pledging their allegiance to William and Mary, so the Earl of Argyll sent his troops, led by the Clan Campbell of Glenlyon, to pay them a call. They stayed a fortnight on the MacDonalds' hospitality, eatin' and drinkin' and having a grand time, and then suddenly they turned on them. Attacked them in their beds and murdered thirty-eight men."

The injustice of it made a flare of anger rise in Juliet's chest. "How horrible. Just for being tardy? Did they mean to pledge their allegiance?" Juliet looked at the rising mountain terrain and imagined the people trying to flee.

"I dinnae ken that any of the clans wanted to pledge to the English, but they had little choice and they knew it. The worst of it is that the soldiers left the women and children to die from the harsh elements." Fiona looked around them as the wind gusted through their hair, and shivered. "The games are here this year to try and restore the goodness of the land."

Juliet thought she could understand that. It was a place to be revered, not sullied by such brutality and bloodshed.

A sudden bellow and then roaring cheers had them turning around toward the wide part of the glen below. A man, shirtless aside from the upper drape of his tartan over one shoulder, his chest heavily muscled, his stance exuding power, stood a head above those around him. He took up a huge object, made a circle and then a lunge and thrust it into the sky. It had a long wooden handle with an iron ball at one end. It flew through the air with the cheers of the crowd and landed halfway down the glen beyond Juliet's sight.

The man turned around, toward them, with a fist upraised, a grin splitting his ruggedly handsome face, his eyes alight with a fierce sort of victory.

Those eyes, so far and yet close enough to make out, scanned past Juliet and Fiona standing above him on the ridge of the road. His gaze swung past them and then came back with sudden determined intent. Juliet gulped. He was staring right at her.

"Is that…?"

Fiona nodded, her voice quiet with awe. "The MacLeon. And he's looking right at you, he is."

"He is?"

"He is."

"Oh dear. What shall I do? Shall I wave? Curtsey?"

Fiona laughed. The bagpipes started up again with a jaunty tune and then the clouds above the MacLeon's head parted, the sun sending a shaft of pure light to bathe him with brightness.

Juliet could only stare and hope her mouth wasn't gaping open. She shut it with a snap and raised her chin, her gaze locked with his.

His mouth turned up in a one-sided grin filled with boyish charm, and his eyes grew mirthful yet intent. He bowed his head toward her and then turned his attention back toward the games.

"Now I ken why my mother wasnae so happy we

were so closely situated to the MacLeon tents." Fiona laughed and squeezed Juliet's hand. "Did she mention that the MacLeon Chief isnae yet married?

"No." Juliet's voice was low and airy. "No, she didn't mention that."

"Aye. And 'tis rumored he is lookin' for a wife."

Chapter Two

"Did you hear what he said, Juliet?" Fiona whispered, and yanked her back away from the opening of the Clan MacLeon tent.

"He wasn't talking about me!" Juliet whispered back, still straining to get closer to hear what the men were saying. "He couldn't have been."

"Who else?" Fiona leaned forward as well to catch more, but the sounds of the deep voices had stopped. "You're the only 'English lass' at the highland games that I know of."

Juliet had to concede that that was true. It was the second day of the games and she had watched Iain MacLeon compete for much of the day and a half that they had been there. They had just been taking a stroll after the midday meal and walking right past the MacLeon encampment when they heard him talking.

Fiona linked her arm to Juliet's and straightened with a mischievous smile. "Let's go have a closer look at him, shall we?"

Juliet's heart began to pound with excitement. "Dare we? Your father said he's the most famed...the most powerful...the most..." She swallowed hard, thinking of his bulging muscles when not an hour ago, he lifted the caber —a twenty-foot wooden pole that must weigh over twelve stone—and threw it the winning distance.

"Exactly." Fiona continued to pull on Juliet's arm. "And he just said that *you* are the bonniest lass at the games."

How he could have thought that, if he was referring to her, was unfathomable. Her mother lamented that her shape was so very "round" and that she lacked the statuesque height and demure features that both her mother and her fair-haired sister shared. Her hair was more red than golden, a bright color that blazed in the sun and drew the eyes of many a man but, unfortunately, not with a wife on their minds. Juliet wasn't entirely sure why she attracted the wrong kind of attention, but her mother was more than displeased by it, demanding large hats and high collars whenever they went in society. And then there was her voice. She shuddered just thinking of it.

Perhaps the chief of Clan MacLeon—Iain Alexander MacLeon. she'd learned—was of that ilk too. Perhaps he thought of her in terms of fire and tempest, not hearth and home.

She ducked her head as Fiona pulled her around the corner of the row of MacLeon tents, staring at the ground and letting her well-meaning—though too brave for sanity's sake—cousin led her down the beaten grass path.

A troupe of pipers came around the other side of the row of tents, a song as old as time beginning from their bagpipes. They marched toward them dressed in their plaids, practicing for the performance to come. Juliet and Fiona froze, both in awe of the drumming and the bagpipes, so close and loud, the knees of the front men kicking against their kilts, the earth pounding beneath their feet. Juliet clutched Fiona's hand, dead in the middle of the path, staring and awestruck, until the pipers were nigh to breathing upon the girls' necks.

They were not going to stop.

They were going to have to do something soon or get stomped beneath God's "Amazing Grace."

Juliet's heart raced as their faces grew closer, knowing she should get out of the way but somehow unable to. The music had cast a spell on her and she couldn't move. It was the most heavenly song she'd ever heard.

"Come on!" Fiona tugged at her arm again, just before their marching feet overtook their frozen, statue-like state.

Fiona might appear a smallish young woman of little strength, but she wasn't anything like that at all. She swung Juliet away from the marching throng, over a patch of grass and into the side of the tent they were standing in front of. The canvas buckled beneath the weight of the two of them, billowing in, caving with a slow kind of deflating and then bouncing them back a bit, but not enough to catch their balance. In they fell again, a sapling pole to their right creaking, then snapping, the sound of tearing fabric as if a big man had just bent over and ripped his drawers.

They both gasped and sputtered as they landed on something hard that was inside the tent. It moved beneath them and they heard a growl. A few shouts sounded from inside the tent against the din of the pipers. Juliet and Fiona looked wide-eyed at each other, hair fallen from their pinned coifs, dresses askew, suppressing horrified mirth.

"Who goes there!" came a thunderous voice, deep and velvety.

All laughter fled and the color drained from both their faces. They disentangled themselves from the canvas, still half on their backs, and looked up at the large man now glaring down at them. Fiona choked back some sort of sound—a half-laugh, half-groan. Juliet swiped the tangled mass of hair from her eyes and saw cross-tied laces of his shoes on thick calves. Her gaze traveled up to a heavy woolen kilt, deep red with green and gold, to a waist with a corded belt, tight with weapons, some sort of knife—broad and glinting in the sun, it made her eyes hurt to look at it. Up her gaze flew to a bare chest, strong, muscled, browned by the sun, arms like….like….

Oh dear Lord in heaven help her, it was *him*.

Her gaze flew to his face, to his eyes. They were blue and mesmerizing in this light, looking at her with such intensity. With his dark blond hair he looked like a lion just awoken from a comfortable nap. His gaze held hers for a long moment, as if she was his prey and he was hypnotizing her into a trap. She shook her head, thinking she was imagining it. Blinking, she tried to rise. He reached out a hand and grasped her arm. She couldn't take her eyes from him, the pipes and drums thrumming in the background lending an unreal cadence to the moment. The chief of the MacLeon pulled her upright. Blue eyes and hair bright like the sun; she couldn't see anything beyond his face and immense chest.

It was the man who had called her "bonny."

"And what do we have here?" His deep voice rumbled against her ear as he drew her close. "Are ya tryin' to cause wreckage upon my humble dwelling or is it just myself yer wantin' to injure?"

"Oh, no, I couldn't possible cause injury to such a, well, that is…" She blinked several times while realizing that Fiona had disentangled herself from the other bit of canvas and was attempting a wavering curtsey, raking her own blond mass back from her forehead. "MacLeon, we meant no harm. Pray forgive us." Fiona sank so low her nose nearly touched the fallen mass of what was left of the right side of his tent. "'Twas an accident, truly—we were about to be trampled by the pipers!"

His gaze swung forward toward the descending backs of the band of the musicians as their music faded toward the main grounds of the festival.

He straightened, squeezed Juliet's arms a little to ascertain she was righted and let go, leaning his head a bit to one side as if to judge if she could manage to stand on her own two feet.

She wasn't sure that she could.

He was so much larger close up—tall and smelling

of a man that had been competing, leather and earth and sweat. Here was a man who was used to ruling and winning with his own bodily strength. A man like none she'd met in London's stuffy ballrooms. A man that made her think of fields worked together, of children wrought beneath covers and born into a tight and loving family, of a strength, a love, that stood the test of time. Of someone who could know her, the real her, and perhaps not mind so very much all her many faults…

Oh, goodness, she had to get control of these wayward thoughts. Those things didn't exist. Women just longed for them.

"Well, lass?" He reached out and rubbed his thumb against her jaw with gentle insistence, demanding that she hold his gaze.

"We were becoming hemmed in by the musicians and jumped aside. My apologies, sir. We meant no harm."

His eyes lit up with curiosity at her words, her voice—which was always low and husky and "filled with a special warmth," as one man had whispered to her, no matter how she tried to make it high and feminine.

One side of his mouth lifted a notch and his eyes

lit with mischievous humor. "But you have done harm. Och, how am I to rest for the hammer throw?" He leaned in and Juliet could see Fiona's eyes to the side of his shoulder grow wide with awe as he said in a low grumble, "What if you cause me to lose, lass?"

"I, uh." Juliet looked up into those startling blue eyes and took a deep breath. "You can't lose," she said in all seriousness. And then lower, with more conviction, "You won't lose."

His serious face transformed movement by movement into a broad grin and then a deep chuckle. "And so I shan't." He bowed to each of them with a nod of his head and then asked, "You'll be my guests, then, the two of you?"

Juliet shot a gaze at Fiona, not sure what he meant.

Fiona's grin filled her whole face as she curtseyed again. Oh dear, she looked to be suppressing that gleeful dance that she did when particularly happy about something. "Do you mean to sit with the MacLeon clan and cheer you on?" Fiona queried with quirked brows. "And we will wave your flag?" she added before he had time to answer.

"Your father willnae mind? He's of the Erskine Clan, is he not?"

Fiona shrugged. "We are not participating in the games this year."

"Ah." He smiled. "Then you have been searching for a clan to champion?"

"Not really, not since we saw y—" Fiona paused when she noticed Juliet's big eyes and shaking head. "Er, yes, we've been watching the opponents."

The chieftain shrugged. "Verra well. If you will champion the MacLeon Clan then all will be forgiven."

The young women exchanged glances.

His gaze then passed over Juliet with a considering eye. "I will find you MacLeon colors to wear. I find I should like to see them on you."

He turned then, and walked away toward the contest fields.

Fiona gasped as soon as he was out of earshot. "Juliet, did you hear that? He wants to see his colors on you!" Fiona grasped both of her upper arms. "It's practically a declaration. Why, he may be going to my father right now to ask for permission to court you."

Juliet took her cousin's hands from her arms. "Or

it could be that he is like many men and only full of disarming charm and wit." She turned her cousin toward the wreckage of the tent. "We should try to fix this."

Fiona looked around the area and then pointed to two men with MacLeon-colored kilts standing nearby, talking and stealing glances that them. "Aye, but we may need some help."

Juliet laughed.

She couldn't help it. If anyone could get the tent fixed without lifting a finger it would certainly be her cheerful blond cousin.

Chapter Three

Iain knelt at the edge of the glen where the greens of the grasses and moss tinged the mountains before and behind him. He closed his eyes and heard the wind's whistle against the rush of a nearby waterfall.

My Lord. My God. Give me wisdom. Put Your words in my mouth.

He tilted his head back and let the sounds fall around him and through him. He breathed in the beauty and felt it enliven him. He opened his eyes.

The colors of the green had changed, always changing depending on the light and the shadow, the mood of the ever-moving clouds above. The highlands. Home of his heart, where the greatest of the Scottish clans had gathered for three days now—feasting and competing and testing the elite among them. It was thus every year, but this year had been different for him. This year he was clan chief and held an English title and lands as well, his father having died a few short months ago.

He'd been well prepared for taking over the clan,

but much had changed since his father's time. After the death of Queen Anne, Scotland had finally agreed to unite with England and signed the Act of Union, uniting them into what they now called Great Britain. Many of the clans were unhappy about it, but their chieftains were also English nobles—having been gifted lands and titles for service to the kings over the centuries. This lead to ever-increasing conflicts of interest, particularly when chieftains were not taking care of their Scottish clans, using the backs of their people for wealthy gain to support their lives as English nobles and members of Parliament in London.

The MacLeon Clan was yet strong, he'd made sure of it. But it was a delicate political line that he walked, trying to keep his people happy while still having to attend Parliament in London and side with the Whigs or the Tories. He didn't particularly ascribe to the passions of either party, choosing to remain as neutral as possible and depending on prayer and the inner voice of God inside him as the occasion demanded.

The weight of it rested heavy at times. Even now there was a man at the games who was hounding him to support a Jacobean rising on behalf of Queen Anne's half-brother, James VIII. There were those who wanted the House of Stuart back on the throne and resisted the Hanoverian George I, who was now crowned king. Iain cared more about improving his clan, bringing in more sheep and finding developments in weaving—a recent interest—than the politics in London.

He rested his head upon one knee and closed his eyes.

"Lord, God, my Father in heaven. Give me this day what is mine, what You have destined as mine and nothing else. Nothing more and nothing less. Let Your will be done here this day for myself and my clan and…"

He paused as a breath of excitement stirred in his heart and the vision of the flame-haired Lady Juliet Lindsay, the daughter of Lord Ashland Lindsay, the Earl of Worland, flashed before him. The deep brightness of her hair shone against the darkness of his closed eyes.

"And as to her, Lord, the clan would not be well pleased with an English wife, especially one so indebted as her father—'tis a reputedly desperate state of affairs—but there is something about her…"

He felt the wind ruffle through his longish hair like a breath from heaven. He lifted his face toward it and exhaled a small laugh, the skin around his eyes feeling tight and crinkling from the hours under the bright sun, knowing God was listening to his heart's longings and confusions, all his prayers. *"And lead me not into temptation."* He chuckled, not wanting to continue the Lord's Prayer with the next line, which would call her evil. *"Your will, not mine. Your will be done."*

As loved by his clan as he was, he had his enemies. And the right bride was just one way to stay ahead of their snarling throats and razor-sharp teeth. An obscure and impoverished English noblewoman would do him little good for those purposes.

Iain stood and took up a large stone like the one he had thrown in the last competition. He lifted it before his eyes and stared at it. He felt the weight in his hand, measured it against the strength in his arm and shoulder and torso. He took a long, even breath, pulled back and heaved it up toward the mountain as hard as he could. The competitions were over and tonight they would have a final feast before they all left for home—and he for Edinburgh, where he hoped to arrange the purchase of fifty sheep to add to his herds.

The sudden sounding of a horn signaled that the feasting was about to begin. Iain rubbed a hand across his prickly chin and turned toward his tents to freshen up before dinner.

~~~~~~

Juliet walked behind Fiona, who was walking behind Aunt Becca, into the cleared area deep within the glen to the sounds of the pipers, drummers and flutes playing. They were wearing their best gowns—Juliet's a deep emerald silk with the MacLeon colors on her chest in the form of a brooch. She and Fiona had fashioned them from a sash that the MacLeon had given them, something that her aunt had frowned over, worry in her eyes, but her uncle had only shrugged his shoulders and said she'd make a right fine Scottish bride. His words had given Juliet a rush of happiness, her cheeks turning pink, but her aunt's obvious worry had tempered her excitement. Perhaps the MacLeon had a reputation as a rake and her aunt was just looking out for her.

She couldn't help but be happy that her hair had turned out so well. Fiona had braided the long length and then wrapped it around her head like a crown. They'd woven purple heather throughout the thick braid, making a pretty contrast with her red hair.

They made their way down into the flat valley of the glen, where there were torches lighting the area against the coming night. Several wooden tables had been pushed together to form a large U, and each clan had its place marked out. The head of the table went to the victors—Clans MacLeon and Cameron, who had won eight and five out of the twenty contests. The other clans were placed on either side of the U, mostly depending on size. Juliet was surprised to find out that their small clan was seated near the head table, right next to Clan MacLeon.

"He's arranged it," Fiona whispered to Juliet with a nod toward Iain. "I'll bet my locket 'e has."

Fiona was always betting her prized gold locket on something or another. Juliet glanced up and saw a tall man, aye, it was the MacLeon, approaching the table wearing his MacLeon kilt and formal dress—a black waistcoat with silver buttons, white shirt with cravat and, hanging in the front of the kilt, a fur sporran with horsehair tassels. He looked magnificent, breathtaking. Their gazes locked. He gave her a nod, admiration in his eyes as his gaze took in her hair and dress. She dipped into a small curtsey, hardly believing he was paying her such heed. Goodness, she was seated only four away from him. How was she to enjoy the feast with him watching her so close and her stomach so knotted up?

The music came to an end while everyone took their seats. Servants scurried to and fro, filling tankards and passing heaping wooden bowls and platters. There was roasted chicken and lamb, haddock and crab claws, cheeses, peas, turnips and carrots, barley bread with butter or raspberry jam and bread pudding and cakes. Fiona, beside her, ate with gusto, as did the rest of the family, but Juliet could hardly enjoy the fine food. She could feel it when his gaze rested on her, like a warm shaft of sunlight in the crisp evening air. She occasionally dared to return the glance, her heart speeding up each time their gazes locked.

"A toast to the victors!" someone to her left shouted, and stood. Everyone cheered and then quieted as he raised his glass. "To Iain of the MacLeon! The victor of the games!"

More cheers went up, with many of the men beating on the tables. Iain was pulled upright from his seat, with men clapping him on the back and shoulders. He seemed uncomfortable with the attention, and yet was laughing and jovial. He made a fist and raised it in victory, the shouts of the crowd egging him on.

Juliet laughed and clapped as well, a strange happiness filling her. Why did she want those strong arms around her so badly? Glancing around and seeing the admiring glances of several of the women made her realize she wasn't the only one. He would pick a wife from one of these, a Scots woman who would be accepted, not an English stranger who represented what so many of them hated. Juliet looked down at her plate and quelled her excitement. Perhaps she could force down the rest of that piece of cake—it was rather good.

She felt a touch on her arm and then heard a deep voice say into her ear, "Will ye have me for the first dance, lass?"

She looked up to see Iain's face, freshly shaven and grinning down at her. "Aye," she heard herself reply. "If you've no fear for your feet. I fear I don't know the Scottish versions of dance."

"'Tis not so different." He leaned closer and took her hand. "I shall show you how."

He had no sooner said that—and Juliet rose beside him—than the tables were being cleared away and pushed back and the musicians gathered on one side with their fiddles, bagpipes, a harp and drums.

With much laughter and teasing, the couples aligned themselves in two rows and awaited the music to begin. It was a jaunty tune that brought a smile to everyone's face. Iain lifted one brow and gave her a nod of encouragement as their set came together, grasped right hands and then passed each other to make up the line on the other side. Juliet had danced a reel before and it was similar, with some different footwork and more pointing of the toes. As she reached for Iain's hand halfway through the dance, she felt she was progressing rather well. Especially considering how sweaty her palms were when he held her hand in his.

The music ended and she resisted the urge to collapse against his wide chest. Before she could say anything, he took her hand and led her to the far side of the dancers. She glanced around nervously, seeing that there were still people milling about and they weren't really alone.

"I shan't take you off into the woods and ravish you, milady," he teased her, leaning back and looking into her eyes.

"Oh"—she felt her face warm—"of course not. I'm just—"

"Protecting your virtue. A noble cause." His voice was velvety smooth and deep. Her face warmed further with the thought of how she had been caught kissing Lord Ardsley in the gardens of a house party in London. She must never put herself in such a position again. The need to tell him the truth, before he expressed any more interest in her, rose quick and strong in her mind. "I've not always guarded it so well."

His brow turned puzzled and his eyes darkened. "No?"

She shook her head and turned away from the piercing stare. "I've a need to be honest with you. I was recently at a ball in London and was convinced to walk through the private gardens by a young man. He, uh…"

"What did he do?" Iain's voice was tense and threaded with anger.

Juliet swung back around to face him. He looked ready to run the man through with a sword. "A kiss is all," Juliet quickly inserted. "But I didn't stop him. We were caught."

"Did he offer for you?" His face remained fierce.

"Yes, he did. But my father rejected his suit. He, uh, wasn't as well situated as my father hopes—hoped—to secure for my hand." She looked down, shame filling her. Her father had thundered his disapproval—not of the kiss itself, but of the man she had allowed to kiss her. Had she chosen to get caught with a wealthy earl or duke, well, that would have been another matter altogether. And her mother had nearly disowned her. In truth, she'd had marks on her face for weeks from her mother's slaps. She didn't know how far her mother would have gone had her brother not jumped in to stop her. Juliet shuddered with the memory.

Iain's hands took hold of her upper arms and pulled her close, his arms wrapping around her. "They punished you, then? Sent you here?"

"Yes." She breathed deep of the woolen tartan across his chest, but dared not move for fear he would take away his comfort.

Surprise filled her when he chuckled, a low rumble against the top of her head. She pulled back. "Is my plight so funny?"

He chuckled again, one side of his mouth up in that boyish look that made him seem younger. "Nay, lass. 'Tis the irony of it."

"What do you mean?"

"They've sent you into far more danger here." His eyes turned dark with teasing promise.

Juliet raised her brows in question. "Have you changed your mind about ravishing me, then?"

"Perhaps I have."

His words sent a thrill through her body, starting at her chest and then pooling down. She suspected her knees might give way if he kept looking at her like that. What would it be like to kiss him? Nothing like the weak peckings from Lord Ardsley, she was sure. All the trouble it had caused and she hadn't even liked it. But with Iain…

He seemed to be considering the same thing as his gaze traveled to her lips. "What sort of kiss did he give ye?" He moved closer, his gaze roving her face, his breath intermingling with hers.

"It was…rather disappointing, I'm afraid." Juliet could hear the huskiness in her voice deepen.

"Was it now?"

She nodded, thrilled and terrified at the same time. What if she was caught again? There were people dancing not far away. They could probably be easily seen, but Iain didn't seem to care. His arm went around her waist and brought her flush with his body. His head lowered, lips parting the least little bit.

They had just touched to hers when a sudden shout and then the sounds of horses galloping interrupted the moment. His gaze jerked to the other side of the dark glen while his body moved to stand in front of her to protect her. He lifted out a long, wicked-looking knife from his belt. Juliet shrank back as two horses came into view. They galloped to a stop in the middle of the glen, where the dancers had stopped and separated.

"Come," Iain demanded, grasping her hand. They hurried to the middle, where the men were dismounting.

Juliet's heart sank when they grew close enough to see the young men's faces. Something must be terribly wrong…one of the men was her brother.

"It's father," Ruck, a nickname for Robert that her brother had inherited as a boy, said as soon as he reached Juliet. "There's been an attack. Father was wounded by an arrow. You must come home at once."

Her aunt gasped, Fiona paled and Juliet's heart lurched in her chest. "Who has done this?"

Her brother looked around at the people crowding to hear and lowered his voice. "They came to collect a debt, threatened to kill us all if they don't have their money by Christmas Day."

"A debt? Is it a mortal wound? How could you leave him?"

Ruck frowned. "It's hard to say. He has a fever but the doctor is seeing to him. I wouldn't have come myself but he insisted. He is asking for you." He lowered his voice further. "Something about a demand for your hand in marriage."

Her hand? In marriage? Her stomach dropped. She had to get home, and as quickly as possible.

"You must go immediately," her Uncle Clyde said by her side. He nodded toward Fiona. "Hurry and pack her things. Becca, some water and food for the journey." He looked over at the tired, heavily breathing horses. "You'll take our horses." He scowled. "I would go with you myself but haven't the stamina to ride as fast as you'll be needin' to go. But I hate to send her off with just the two of you young lads."

"We met with no trouble on our journey here," Ruck assured him. "The fresh horses are much appreciated."

"Yes, but still..." He looked over at the smallish servant who had accompanied Ruck. "I'd feel better if I could see her safely home myself." His frown deepened.

"I'll accompany them."

All eyes swung toward Iain. Juliet's eyes widened in shock.

"I have business in Edinburgh and was planning to travel to the south after the festival. It will only be a little out of the way to accompany them to Northumberland first and see to Edinburgh on my way back home."

Uncle Clyde's face lit up. "MacLeon, you are too generous, but I gladly accept your offer. I will sleep well knowing my niece is in safe hands with you escorting her."

Ruck made a noise in his throat but didn't say anything, just stared at the tall MacLeon chief.

Juliet found herself relieved. Ruck was three years younger than she at seventeen, and the servant he'd brought along looked to be about his same age and dropping off to sleep. To have a man, a man skilled at battle and knowledgeable of the land and any dangers therein, would be fortunate indeed.

She looked over at him and saw determination in his eyes, determination and something else—protectiveness? She took a deep breath, not breaking contact with his eyes. It was a new feeling to realize that she had such strength, a fierce loyalty, at her side. How could it be? They'd only known of each other for three days. She didn't understand it, but whether they liked it or not, there was something between them that would not be denied.

Within the hour, the four of them were riding out of the glade into the night.

Chapter Four

A chill wind blew Juliet's hair out of its knot at the back of her head, leaving it to flail about her shoulders and across her face as they trotted through the tall, black iron gates and into the city of Edinburgh. The town had an ancient, haunted feel to it, the smokestacks on every building bellowing smoke so much so that the stone had turned black in places on the buildings. But it was as if an artist's brush had directed the smoke—the patterns in the stone added depth and character to the otherwise white sandstone. Rows upon rows of connected houses and shops and pubs with spectacular, gothic cathedrals taking up huge corners of the streets. She must have stepped back in time it seemed, to the ancient days of knights and dragons and folklore of days long past.

Her horse, Lisbeth, trotted with eagerness up the cobblestone street, sensing food and rest was soon to come. To their left stood the mighty fortress that was Edinburgh Castle, a formidable military stronghold that had been there for centuries. Built on the top of an ancient volcano, its stones jutted from the land as if it had sprouted up out of it.

Juliet shielded her eyes, her gaze wandering over to its many buildings and walls. There was a military force there now, Iain had told them. A militia that had supported Queen Anne and now George I. Her father, if his Jacobean leanings were discovered, would be considered a threat and an enemy. Iain had assured them that they would stay clear of the castle and Holyrood Palace, another colossal—though more modernized and lived-in—castle on the eastern end of the Royal Mile, where nobles held residences in the Queen's Apartments. But this was not a time to see such things. They were in Edinburgh for a brief rest after three days of hard traveling and to stock up on badly needed supplies.

The deeper they rode into the city the more Juliet was fascinated by it, even though the smoke from the many chimneys, filling the air with a sharp peat smell, burned her nose. It was ghastly and haunting and stunning all at once.

"Will you arrange for your sheep while we are here?" Juliet asked Iain when their horses slowed to a side-by-side walk.

"Nay, we shan't tarry, lass. I will have time for that on my return."

He hadn't said much to her over the past days. None of them had talked about much of anything except at the necessary stops. Twice they slept for a few hours, out in the open and in a circle around a small fire. The only other times they stopped were if they came upon a stream or loch, to replenish their water and stretch their legs. Every muscle in Juliet's body screamed at her when she dismounted and tried to walk. She was more than thankful she and Fiona had taken daily rides, or she never would have kept up on such a lengthy journey.

"Here." Ian motioned them to turn down a narrow lane that soon became steep. A little ways down he led them to the back of a coaching house where they could pay to have their horses fed and tended to.

Next to the carriage house was a lodging house with a long common room. They found a table with four chairs, Juliet twisting up her hair into a semblance of a knot while they walked inside, and sat down. The landlord came over with four tankards and quickly filled them.

"Meat pie today." He bowed toward Iain. "You can have bread trenchers if you like."

"Aye, four of them, if you please. And are their beds available? We aim to catch a few winks before continuing our journey."

The man looked around the table at the four of them. "One bed, but I might be able to arrange somethin' for the lady. Where are you heading?"

"The lady has been visiting cousins in Scotland. We've been assigned with her safe passage back to Northumberland."

"Oh, Northumberland, is it now? There's been some trouble there, I heard. Some of that Jacobean business." He turned and spat on the floor. Juliet turned her head away.

"Yes, we've heard. We'll not be traveling there. A hunk of cheese will do us well, if you have it." He changed the subject and the man rushed off to do his bidding.

Juliet breathed a sigh of relief as Iain reached beneath the table and squeezed her hand.

Several moments later, as they were deep into their meat pies, a dozen or so soldiers entered the inn. Juliet could feel Iain's body tense beside her. His gaze took in the soldiers and then he turned his back on them and murmured, "Finish up, lads, 'tis time to find our beds." He leaned toward her brother and said in a quiet voice, "You lads take the bed here. Three hours' rest and then I will come and fetch you. I'll be finding yer sister a place to rest nearby."

They hurriedly finished their meal, Ruck and his servant, Joseph, heading up the stairs to the room they were given. Iain kept Juliet next to him for several more minutes, their backs to the soldiers with a hand over hers under the table. They listened to the talk and heard the words "Jacobite scum" more than once. "Keep your head down and follow me," he whispered.

She nodded, pulling the hood of her cloak over her head.

Instead of going toward the main door, which would put them near the soldiers, Iain led her by the hand to the back of the common room towards the kitchen. Without a word to anyone, he pulled her through the busy kitchen and out a back door, and then drew her close to his side. They were in a tight little alleyway with many-storied buildings crowding them on either side.

"Where are we going?" Juliet whispered, looking around at the poor, crowded lodgings and dimly lit street, a stream of sewage running next to the road.

"I know of a safe place where we can get some rest. It's just down this way." He kept her hand and guided her over the uneven cobblestones to a building with a blue door. He went in without knocking and Juliet quickly followed, blinking in the sudden darkness to adjust her eyes.

A happy shriek and then a woman propelled herself into them, stepping on Juliet's foot.

"Ouch," Juliet squeaked.

The woman barely noticed her. "Iain, my darlin' Iain. Why have you been so long from us?" She kissed him square on the mouth and then let out a low laugh.

Iain set her away from him with that disarming smile. "Molly, good to see you, lass. This is Lady Lindsay. I've volunteered to see her safely home and we could use a bed for a few hours of rest before we take ourselves back to the road. Might you have something?"

Molly looked at Juliet as if she were a vile insect.

"Where is Daniel? Is he at home?"

Molly waved that away. "'E's never home this time of day, that husband of mine. You know how 'e is." She looked back at Juliet. "If you'll stay while she sleeps and keep me company, I'll see what I can do." She lifted her brows at Iain.

Who was this woman? A dalliance? A past lover? She was a married woman. Juliet couldn't fathom what their relationship could be.

"I was thinking of sleeping on the floor next to her,

truth be told." Juliet heard the weariness of the journey in his voice. "We've been traveling nigh on three days and I wouldn't mind a few winks before we continue."

"Och, you poor dear. All right, then, follow me."

She lead them up a narrow stone staircase to a third floor, down a short hall and into a tiny room with a bed, a table with a candle and some hooks on the wall, with a cloudy mirror beside them. "Just hang your things there. You know where to find me if you change your mind." She sing-songed the last toward Iain.

Iain shut the door, his face a telling shade of red.

"Who was that?"

"Her husband is an old friend, from childhood. He claims she married him to get close to me, which I dinnae believe."

"You don't? She practically threw herself at you just now."

"It's just her way."

Juliet let out a "humph" but was too exhausted to argue. It wasn't her business anyway.

She hung her fur cloak on the hook and sat on the bed. Mmmm, a real feather bed with down pillows and clean sheets—heaven. While taking off her shoes she saw Iain shrug out of his outer coat and hang it next to hers. He leaned back his head, closed his eyes and stretched. His eyes looked tired, and Juliet was filled with remorse for thinking ill of him. She should be more thankful, especially after hearing those men in the coaching house. Her brother and their servant wouldn't have known what to do if things had turned ugly there. She hated the thought of their faithful guide sleeping on the hard floor.

"If you'd like to sleep on the bed we can roll up that blanket on the end there and place it between us."

His eyes held hers, weighing the idea, then his mouth curved into a half-grin. "So, 'tis a temptress you are, then?"

Juliet let out a laugh. "Not to be compared to the likes of Molly, but…" She grinned back and mimicked Molly's Scottish brogue, "It may be that I'm takin' notes, *Iain*."

It was the first time she had called him by his given name, and it somehow hadn't come out like Molly said his name at all. It had come out like she usually talked, only even huskier, her feelings for him lacing the words, making them low and raspy, rich and wanting. Her face grew warm.

Iain groaned, took one pillow from the bed and the extra blanket from the foot of the bed and lay down on the floor. Juliana leaned over the side of the bed and peered at him, seeing him straighten the kilt that had risen to mid-thigh and stretch out the blanket. He turned away from her and she lay back down, sighing and closing her eyes.

"Ye are far more potent than she, lass." His voice grew even fainter, as if he would drop off into sleep at any moment. Then he murmured, "Much too potent for the likes of me."

She smiled and dozed off, as happy and exhausted as she'd ever been.

~~~~~~~

It was nearing nightfall as the foursome trotted into the small village of Ennis, just outside the Lindsay lands and Eden Place. Juliet scanned the village, noting the poor condition of the houses and strained faces of the villagers who were coming out of their homes and shops. Their foursome was greeted with dour faces and shouts: "What's to become of us, milady?" And, "Yer father, milady, is he yet alive? We hear he's gravely ill."

Juliet shot a look over at her brother. Ruck's eyebrows pulled together in a frown. "He was healing from the arrow wound when I left for you.

Perhaps it has taken infection. We must hurry."

They raced down the narrow lane and came to the iron gates of the Lindsay estate. Joseph dismounted to open them.

Iain came alongside her and said in a low voice, "Milady, we should pray. We know not what we are about to encounter, but God knows all and is with us."

Juliet felt her pulse quicken. "I fear I should warn you…my parents, they aren't the sort to gain God's favor. They aren't anything like Uncle Clyde and Aunt Becca."

Iain smiled a kind smile at her, his eyes full of warmth. "We none of us deserve God's favor—'tis a gift he chooses to bestow on whomever He wishes."

"It matters not if you are good or bad?"

"It matters to those who are good and bad to this realm, yes. But God sees into the hearts of men and judges with a wisdom we cannot fathom. That is why we must trust in His ways."

Juliet let that thought sink in while the servant remounted his horse. When Ruck started to proceed through the gates, Juliet stopped him. "A moment, Ruck. The MacLeon wishes to pray."

Her brother looked startled but reigned in his horse. They all bowed their heads.

"Dear Father." Iain's deep voice said the words as to a dearly loved parent. "We come before Thee not leaning on our own understanding but asking You for Your wisdom and guidance in this matter with Lord Lindsay and these challenges before us. We pray that if it be Your will you will strengthen and heal Lord Lindsay from his wounding and that You will guide and protect him from his enemies. Pray, give us the strength to endure all that is to come. Amen."

"Amen," they all echoed.

Juliet felt an odd calm come over her and looked over at Iain with an ever-deepening respect. She had never heard a man—especially such a strong and powerful man of the nobility—humble himself like that before, admitting in front of others that he didn't know what to do and needed help. Instead of taking anything away from him, it made him seem even more a leader, strong and desirable.

They rode down the long stone path to the palatial home where Juliet had grown up. Made of pink granite, the three-story edifice had seven large windows across every floor, two on either side of the front columned façade and three in the middle above the double doors. A servant came out and took their horses, his face down as if he couldn't look them in the eye. Joseph disappeared with the horses toward the stables.

Juliet ran up the wide stone steps to the front door and hurried inside, the men just behind her.

"Thank heaven, you're here." Nettie, their long-time housekeeper completed a perfunctory curtsey towards the three of them and hurried on. "Yer father, he be on 'is last breath. Hurry, my lords, my lady." She gazed at Iain with widening eyes, taking in his tartan and large frame.

"Nettie, this is the chief of the Clan MacLeon, from Scotland. He has been so kind as to guide us home. Would you see to his comfort while Ruck and I see Father?"

The maid nodded.

"Where's Mother?" Ruck asked, heading for the winding staircase on the left side of the large entry hall.

"Heaven only knows. She's not gone near your father since the putrid smell began. The wound seeps horribly."

"Lady Lindsay." Iain's voice stopped her. "I would accompany you to see your father if you wish. I have some knowledge of battle wounds and would like to see what the physician is doing for him."

Juliet waved him to follow them. "Of course. Follow me."

She led the way up three flights of stairs and down a long, shadowed hall. Juliet saw the place as Iain must see it—shabby and ill kept, the carpets old and worn, bare wall where paintings used to hang, the sconces on the walls rusted and sooty—but it did little good to be embarrassed about it. Her father wasn't a good estate manager, had led them into ruin if the truth be known, and there was nothing she could do to hide the plain facts around them.

They could smell her father's illness before opening the door. Juliet held her sleeve over her nose and opened it. Her father lay in the large four-poster bed, the bed hangings drawn on the side of the widows. Ruck made a sound from his throat but took Juliet's hand and walked with her toward him.

Her father turned his head at the sounds of their approach. Juliet faltered, a cry coming from her throat. He looked so thin, so pale, with a greenish tinge. Her gaze traveled to his shoulder, where an angry red swelling of putrid flesh oozed around a gaping hole covered in a mash of some sort of poultice. Her stomach rolled as she took shallow breaths and came to his side.

"Father, what's happened?"

Her father looked over her head at Iain and frowned, but only for a moment, and then rasped out, "You've come in time. As you can see...I'm dying. James will have to take back the throne without me."

How could he think of the deposed king on his deathbed didn't bear contemplation to her. "Is it an infection?"

Her father cursed and then wheezed, coughing to catch his breath, the rattle in his lungs none too good. "They've bled me to death trying to get rid of the bloody infection, but it's taken over my body. I can feel its grasp tightening. It won't be long now."

"Father," Ruck said brokenly.

Her father's gaze swung toward her brother and then back to her, ignoring him. He scowled. "Your only hope is a wealthy marriage. After your"—he gasped for breath and then rallied, determination lighting his eyes—"debacle at that blasted ball we had little hope, but I've found one man willing to take you." He paused again for breath. "Lord Richard Malcolm." His voice was laced with a feverish glee as he said the name.

Juliet's heart froze. She was unable to speak. Lord Malcolm's face came into focus behind her closed eyes. A stern, thin face with beady eyes and a long, pointed nose. He was at least sixty and known as a Jacobean zealot and cruel master. His third wife had killed herself after only two years of marriage. Juliet could not believe her father would even consider such a thing. A trembling began at her knees and moved up her body. She started to collapse, but Iain caught her and held her upright by one arm.

"Father, no," she gasped out, "I could never—"

"You can and you will!" her father shouted, shocking them all. "If you don't, by Christmas Day, you will all lose everything. Your mother and brother and sister will have nowhere to live. They will be slaves or prisoners in the debtor's gaol. Juliet, you have no choice. I've already promised him. He has already paid the debts!"

Juliet shook her head and backed away. "No, I cannot."

Her father fell back onto his pillow and closed his eyes. "You have no choice," he whispered. "Leave me."

Juliet turned and ran from the room.

Chapter Five

Dinner was a stark event.

Stark decorations in a stark dining room. Stark food upon a stark table. Leaden hearts showing on stark faces. A stark event indeed.

Iain repeated his earlier prayer to keep himself from snatching Juliet up and whisking her home to Scotland. What he would do with her once he got her there he didn't want to think about. Marry her? Much of him, the man that he was, wanted her as wife, but he could not bring home an English bride. His clan would not tolerate her, and her life would be as stark as this room without their approval. And yet, he thought as he looked over at her ashen face, how could he leave her to this Lord Malcolm? A man he had heard of himself as a monster. He had spent the past hour in the drawing room with Ruck telling him of even more. It was a fate he couldn't imagine for Juliet, and yet he must not act out of emotion. He had to wait and listen for God's way of escape. It was a delicate balance that he'd had to practice before, but with a woman involved—this woman—he was finding it harder than anything he had ever done.

"We must thank you again, Lord MacLeon, for seeing our Juliet home to safety. I dreaded sending Ruck with only a servant, but as you can see, we've fallen on difficult times and there was no one else," Juliet's mother said with a pinched face.

Iain had only seen a handful of servants on the estate and had no reason to doubt her words. "'Twas my pleasure," he replied in a low voice.

"Shall you return to Scotland directly, then?" She took a tiny bite of her meat and chewed it for a long time. Juliet's mother, Hermione, had blond hair threaded with gray and a rail-thin body, with an equally thin voice. Juliet's younger sister, Claire, had the look and mincing actions of her mother, but still the glow of youth, while Juliet had inherited the richer coloring of her father and lush curves. He noted that Juliet ate her meal with the enthusiasm of someone who was active and hearty, though her curvaceous figure was that of a full-grown woman. She was the type who wouldn't shy away from hard physical labor but could dress up and turn the eyes of any man at a ball or opera, especially once she spoke with that velvety voice of hers. Just the thought of how she had said his name made the blood rush to places unseemly for the dinner table. He forced his thoughts in another direction, answering her mother.

"I've business in Edinburgh to attend to, and then home."

"Juliet tells me your home is in the highlands? Is it a remote area?"

"Aye, and the most beautiful place in the world. I've inherited Eilean Donan, a castle built on an island on Loch Duich. It lies where three lochs come together with mountains to the east and north."

"Aren't there Jacobean sympathizers in the highlands?" Hermione asked, ignoring his poetic description.

"Aye. There are those, ma'am."

"You are not among them?" Her thin brows rose halfway upon her forehead.

"I've a mind more to improving my land and the plight of my people."

"But surely you have a side. Are you Catholic?"

"I prefer the title of Christian." He was about to turn the topic of conversation to something less volatile when the housekeeper burst into the room. Tears streamed down her wrinkled face.

"He's gone, milady. Lord Lindsay is dead."

~~~~~~~

Rain fell in sheets along with a gusting wind as Juliet, Iain, her family and some servants and villagers stood around the grave where her father was being laid to rest. The clergyman read from the Psalms, but Juliet took little comfort in the words. All she could think of were two words.

Christmas Day.

She had to find a way to save their home and pay back Lord Malcolm, whom she had learned had indeed paid off her father's astounding debts in exchange for her hand in marriage. What was she to do? It was just shy of two months away.

Her mother's words from earlier that morning haunted her. Juliet closed her eyes and saw her mother's angry face. Harsh and furious…crying and railing against her.

"If only you'd done what I told you. You've ruined everything."

Her mother's long, thin hair covered, for a moment, her bent head, and then she raked it back with a wrinkled hand, lifted her head and stared at Juliet with such hated that it had robbed her of all her breath. She took a step backward, not wanting to be in her mother's bedchamber, with those thick damask bed-hangings around a bed and heavy curtains blocking any light.

What *had* she done? Had one kiss with a handsome stranger really ruined her? It seemed unfair and impossible, but of that everyone, her mother first and foremost, seemed convinced.

Ruined.

No one would want her now. That was what they all said. Was it true?

Now, she stood at her father's gravesite and thought of Iain's prayer. She repeated it as best as she could remember. If God would help her, perform some miracle and save her from this horrible fate, she would never doubt His love for her again. But it seemed impossible.

As she lifted her head she heard the sounds of horses' hooves, and turned. Two men in long black capes were trotting toward them, rain dripping from their wide-brimmed hats. Juliet squinted, her heart dropping to her stomach as their faces came into focus. Lord Malcolm. She turned quickly away, back toward her father's grave. How could he have done this to her? Her parents were the most selfish, unloving... Her body trembled with fear and dread and anger.

"Hush, lass," Iain's voice sounded deep beside her ear. "I willnae let them take you." He moved closer, put her hand on his arm and placed his large, warm hand over hers, the rain soaking their sleeves.

She looked up into Iain's intense blue eyes. Would he not? What could he really do to protect her? She was legally bound. But hope still sprang in her chest. Perhaps she could run away, go back to Uncle Clyde and Aunt Becca's and quietly live in Scotland. Even as she thought it, her gaze swung to Ruck and Claire and her mother. They would be kicked out into the streets, possibly into debtor's prison. She couldn't let that happen, no matter that there was little love lost between her mother and her. Claire was only fourteen and Ruck just on the cusp of being a man. She couldn't let them suffer for what their father had done. But she could not marry Lord Malcolm either. It was unthinkable.

She felt and heard, more than saw, Lord Malcolm and the man with him dismount and walk over to her mother. The clergyman had finished his prayer and all eyes watched as Lord Malcolm's thin frame swept into a bow toward her mother, murmuring his apologies in a high, overly cultured voice that made Juliet's skin crawl. He turned next toward Juliet and swept toward her like the grim reaper, his black cape gusting with the wind.

Juliet instinctively tightened her grip on Iain's arm and stepped closer to his side. Lord Malcolm's face tightened into a deep scowl. He stood eye to eye with Iain for a long moment and then bowed toward Juliet.

"Milady, my sincere condolences on the death of your father. You must be devastated."

"Yes, my lord, for many reasons."

His scowl deepened and his eyes shot venom. "Won't you introduce your…friend?"

"This is the MacLeon of the Clan MacLeon of Eilean Donan. He was kind enough to escort my brother and me home."

The two men stared again at each other. "Kindness is a valued virtue in our friends, is it not? Though I doubt that particular notion guided him. Loyalty, though…" he wheezed with a cough. "I insist on it from my friends, and most particularly from my wife." His beady gaze swung back to Iain. "*Kindly* take your hands off my betrothed."

Juliet's mother rushed to intervene. "My lord, let us all get out of this rain and attend to the dinner we have planned." She took hold of Lord Malcolm's arm, which he promptly jerked out of her hand, an action she ignored, and then she waved them all toward the manor house.

Juliet kept a tight grip on Iain's arm as they made their way toward the front entrance. Lord Malcolm may as well know that he would not be getting any loyalty out of her.

After they had all dried off the best they could, they regrouped in the drawing room near the two fireplaces, trying to warm themselves and dry out while the meal was getting some last touches. Juliet sipped from the cup of warm mulled wine and turned the dampest section in the back of her skirts toward the fire. Iain had left her side to join the men on the other side of the room, whispering, "Fear not," and giving her hand an encouraging squeeze.

"I'll not have you ruining this union, Juliet," her mother hissed at her as soon as Iain left.

"I won't marry him."

"You must. Do you have any idea what will happen to all of us if you refuse? It's your own fault Lord Malcolm was the only one to offer for you…after that ravishment in the garden."

"A kiss is hardly—"

"Don't think to tell me about society's rules, young lady. You could have had any number of wealthy men but you had to destroy any chance—" She looked ready to burst into tears and then rallied. "Do you think I like this? Do you think I'm so heartless? He's a stingy miser and cruel. He wasn't my first choice for a son-in-law, I can tell you, but you've made all our beds and now we have to lie in them."

How could her mother say such things? Juliet felt tears prick her eyes and forced them back. It had only been a small kiss. She hadn't really even enjoyed it, had just let the curiosity of the moment carry her away. What *had* she done? Maybe that was why Iain, even though there was an obvious attraction between them, hadn't mentioned a union between the two of them. That and the fact that she was English. They were doomed from the start.

Her gaze wandered over to where he stood, the tallest man in the room, with longish, dark blond hair tied back in a queue, and proudly wearing his red tartan kilt. She'd never known a man in a kilt could be so attractive, but he was—particularly in comparison to the men standing in their drawing room. He nigh took her breath away.

Comparing that glorious vision with the dark, thin Lord Malcolm made her stomach roll in revulsion. *Dear God, I cannot marry that man! Help me, please!*

Their housekeeper came in and announced dinner was to be served. The men would usually pick a female to escort into the dining room by offering her his arm. Juliet panicked when she saw both Iain and Lord Malcolm coming toward her. Her brother went by and she leapt at the chance to avoid further conflict by grasping his arm. "Escort me in, Ruck."

Ruck noted the scowl on Lord Malcolm's face and grinned. "My pleasure, sis." He whisked her out of the room as if her skirts were on fire. "You can't marry him, you know."

"I know!" she whisper-hissed. "But what am I to do?"

"I should marry an heiress, and then you wouldn't have to sacrifice yourself."

"You are too young, and besides, it would take time to arrange such a match—time we do not have."

"I heard of man who kidnapped himself an heiress. He and his friends smuggled her out of her bed, took her off to Gretna Green and married her before her parents knew she had even left the house. Perhaps I can find a young lady thirsting for such an adventure." His grin widened at the thought.

"Ruck, don't be ridiculous. I doubt the young lady's father would be in the mood to pay off our debts to Lord Malcolm under such conditions."

He shrugged, pulling back a chair for her toward the head of the table by her mother. "Suppose not. Wait." He nodded toward Iain. "The MacLeon is mad for you. Why not we kidnap him? We could do it tonight, whilst he sleeps."

"Have you lost your head?" Juliet gasped with a half-laugh despite the dire circumstances. The thought that they could make Iain do anything he didn't want to do was just too…unimaginable.

"Thank about it, sis. We could slip a little of that laudanum that mother uses into his after-dinner drink. I'll coax him off to bed early, you stay and entertain old Malcolm to throw him off, and then we'll load him into the carriage once everyone is asleep. We could make Gretna Green in about three hours if we push. He'll be waking up right in time to say the vows and—"

"And why do you suppose he would say vows? If he wanted me as his bride he would have asked."

"Nay, he's over the moon for you, anyone can see that. He just needs a little nudge to get beyond the idea of an English wife. Why, if he was forced then his clan couldn't be too mad at 'im, could they?"

A little nudge. Did she want a husband that had to be threatened or tricked or even nudged into marrying her? And the clan might forgive him, but they would never forgive her if they learned of such scheming to have their chieftain. It was ludicrous to even think such thoughts.

"Ruck, sit down. Whatever are you up to, whispering to your sister like that?" Their mother's gaze shot scorn at the two of them, making Juliet's face heat with embarrassment. Ruck slipped into his chair down at the other end of the table, but not before winking at her before he turned his attention elsewhere.

Juliet looked down at the plate of food in front of her and covered her mouth with one hand. She closed her eyes, her breath heavy in her chest, the bright conversation all around her loud and intrusive. She longed for the quiet of her bedchamber, the stone floor hard and sharp against her knees. She pictured herself kneeling in prayer.

God? Could it be? Could this strange and desperate idea be the answer? It couldn't, and yet…show me the way.

Chapter Six

Iain nodded at Ruck and took another drink from the tankard that Ruck kept insisting was the best ale in Northumberland. Was the lad trying to get him too deep into his cups to leave on the morrow? He'd told him that he had to leave for Edinburgh—business with the sheep he had, but that he would come back and see to his sister, and…well, he shook his head as if to clear it. He'd promised to come back is all, he hadn't said what he would do when he got back to Eden Place because he wasn't exactly sure what he could do.

He shook his head again and closed his eyes. They wanted to close and not open again…and his speech…he could feel it. He was slipping into the deep Scottish brogue of the highlands that few but his fellow Gaelics could understand. He was just so bone weary…God help him.

He rubbed his hand across his face and felt the prickle of two days' worth of beard. He needed a good shave and a warmed towel on his face, that was what he needed. And a nice, soft bed…

"MacLeon, did you hear me?"

Iain swung toward the voice. It sounded close and yet echoed as if down in a deep gorge. The room began to sway. *Good God in heaven*, he prayed, *what have I drunk to feel so?* He was exhausted to the point of wanting to fall on the floor in a full snore. He waved at the voice, not caring if it was Malcolm, and then looked for Ruck. Where was that young pup? He'd show him his bed or see the blunt side of his—

Ruck appeared at his side. "Come, MacLeon. I've something important to show you."

Iain sincerely hoped it was a thick feather pillow.

They made their way up the winding stone stairs to the third floor, where the bedchambers lay against each side of a long and narrow hall. Ruck guided him with rough nudges in the right direction, opened a door and pushed him inside.

The lad needn't be so pushy. The glowing light of the moon came in from tall windows and lit the room. A large, four-poster bed beckoned like a long-lost lover.

"Sleep." He felt the word thick from his lips. "Just some—"

"Yes." Ruck's voice was like a mother's gentle

nudging. "You just need some sleep." Just like his mother used to say when he was sick with the fever.

He fell across the bed and half helped while Ruck took off his shoes. The boy slung his legs up onto the bed and then covered him with a nice-smelling blanket. He had to acknowledge that even though Juliet's home had long been pillaged of its riches, it smelled better than most and was very comfortable. He rubbed his face against the coverlet's softness, feeling like a young lad and thinking this bed was a distant piece of heaven.

"Good eventide to you, MacLeon." Ruck's shadow bowed toward him as it backed away.

"Wait." Iain rallied for a moment and turned his head toward the lad. "Yer sister…" He blinked heavily. So…very…tired…

"Aye?"

Iain rolled onto his back and flung his arms out wide, taking a long, deep breath. "Ya know I love 'er, dinnae ya, lad?"

Iain heard a soft chuckle. "Aye, MacLeon. I'm counting on it."

He heard the soft thud of the door closing and then darkness closed all around him.

~~~~~~

"Juliet!"

"Juliet, wake up!"

Juliet turned from the sound, always being a deep sleeper, and tried to bury her head under her pillow.

"Juliet, if you don't want to find yourself the bride of Malcolm in the morn then you had better wake up!"

She reared up, breathing fast and blinking awake. "What?"

"Shhhh!"

She turned to see Ruck standing at the side of her bed with a flickering candle. "He's out cold. The plan's worked."

"Plan?"

"Juliet! The MacLeon. I gave him a little more than what I think Mother usually has at night to help her sleep. It must have been enough. He's snoring loud enough to wake the dead."

"You went through with it? Oh, may the Lord have mercy upon us! I never agreed to your daft plan! Are you mad?"

"He said he loves you." Ruck took a step back and pursed his lips together, waiting. Her brother knew he had just played his winning card, the only card that might change her mind. Even knowing that didn't change the sudden springing in her heart region. "How do you know?"

"He told me." Ruck struck a slack face and mimicked the Scottish brogue: "Ya know I love 'er, dinnae ya, lad?"

"He said that?" Juliet sprang from the bed and grasped her dressing gown, throwing it over her shoulders and tying the blue satin ribbons up the bodice, dressing faster than she'd ever gotten dressed.

Ruck grinned and Juliet groaned. "He did."

"Ruck, this is madness. I know you want to help and everyone knows I need something, some plan, but to drug and kidnap a Scottish chief and then expect him to take vows—"

"It'll work, Juliet. I know it will."

Juliet looked at her brother and felt tears prick from behind her eyes. This time she didn't try to push them away, and let them fall. They had just lost their father and now had to deal with Lord Malcolm—no wonder they were grasping at straws. "Show me to him. I just need to know you haven't given him too much."

Ruck made a disgruntled noise but led her out her room and toward the bedchamber he had given to Iain.

When they passed the top of the stairs, loud voices stopped them in their tracks. They shrank back against the wall, back into the shadows.

"There's no sense in waiting, my lord. We should take the girl with us in the morning, as soon as the Scotsman has left, and avoid any trouble with the MacLeon. You've the marriage contract signed by Lord Lindsay—why wait for them to delay it with scheming and trickery?"

"Yes, why wait for that delicious flesh in my bed?" A hollow-sounding chuckle filled the room, joined by the bawdy laughter of Lord Malcolm's men. A chair scraped as if they were leaving the table.

Juliet felt the blood leave her face. They would take her, by force, tomorrow morning. Her mother would do nothing to stop them. No one would. She gripped her hands together so tightly that she felt the pain of it enter her consciousness. Ruck grasped her arm and pulled her down the hall, his finger to his lips, reminding her to be quiet.

They entered a back bedchamber used for guests, though rarely, and Ruck gently closed the door. Moonlight flooded the room from the two paned-glass windows. Juliet turned and saw Iain, asleep and deeply snoring, on the bed. He was still wearing his attire of the evening, save his leather shoes and laces.

"Hurry." Her brother motioned her toward the bed. "We have no choice now. Help me get his shoes back on."

Juliet moved as if wooden and yet obedient. Her brother, her dear brother she had always loved and cared for, was taking charge and taking care of her. She hardly knew what she was doing as she laced his shoes up his lean but muscled calves. She glanced at his face, relieved he was breathing normally and yet glad he slept so soundly. Ruck had given him plenty of laudanum for their purposes.

"He's so much bigger than we are. How are we to get him to the carriage?"

Ruck shoved the other shoe into her hands and then went to the dressing chamber and pulled out a long board with a strap attached in the middle. Juliet recognized it. It was used upon occasion when someone was injured, or someone had shot a large animal, when something large had to be carried. "Ruck, I can't possibly carry one side of that. He must weigh twelve stone."

"We can, dear sister, and we will. Just think of Malcolm's bed and you'll be strengthened."

She had to admit that the thought gave her the courage to at least try.

They propped one end of the board against the bed and slung Iain's legs over it. With Juliet at his head and Ruck pulling from Iain's waist, they managed to get him mostly on top of it. He only snored all the louder.

"Wait, I have an idea." Juliet stopped Ruck before he tried to lift an end. She went to the water closet and took out two casks of wine, remembering that they stored some in this guestroom. They were wooden and mostly round. "If we put them beneath the board, and then roll him, moving the casks as needed, we can at least get him to the head of the stairs with little sound."

Ruck nodded, his mouth turning up in a grin. "Good thinking."

It worked rather well. They paused at the door to make sure their guests had retired for the night and heard no sounds, only seeing the faint flicker of a candle someone had left burning in the great room.

At the top of the stairs they paused and looked at each other. Now what?

"Too bad we can't just roll him down the stairs," Ruck whispered.

Juliet held back a hysterical laugh. She still felt like she was an actor in a play. Her life really hadn't come to this, had it?

"Well, if we both get on the lower end, we might, mightn't we?"

Ruck nodded. "Be careful. He won't be happy if we dump 'im down the stairs and he wakes all bruised."

Juliet paled to even think of his reaction should they harm him. "All right. Just remain quiet."

"Of course, come on."

Juliet took one side of the board while Ruck took the other at Iain's feet. Slowly, they slid him, step by step down the staircase.

At the bottom they both looked up longingly at the wine casks. "Go up and get them." Juliet nodded at Ruck.

A sudden noise from the great room, right around a corner and to their right, made them both freeze. A man groaned and moved.

They pulled back into the shadows but couldn't begin to move the board or Iain, who was still softly snoring. Juliet reached over and held her hand to his mouth, but that only made the snore come out his nose with a soft snuffling sound.

Oh dear.

"Someone's coming!" Ruck whispered. "Quick, we have to move him." Ruck took a shoulder and pushed him upright. Juliet went around to the other shoulder and together they heaved him to his feet. He wasn't completely unconscious once they moved him about, so he was able to stand, or rather sway, on his feet. They each put one of his arms around their shoulders and half dragged, half carried him around the stone corner toward the entry. Hopefully, whoever was walking around the great hall wouldn't notice the board at the foot of the stairs.

With his feet barely shuffling and sometimes sliding behind him, they managed to get him outside, where Juliet collapsed against the weight. "I can't go another step," she whispered.

Ruck let the other side down and propped Iain against a stone column. "Let's drag him back into those bushes. You sit with him and I'll fetch the carriage.

"Mother is going to strangle us for this."

"We'll say it was the MacLeon's idea. You're not at fault." Ruck grinned, his eyes so bright with adventure in the moonlight that Juliet felt a pang of love for her brother. She nodded for him to go, but kept wondering.

What would become of them all?

Chapter Seven

Iain woke to the jolting of a carriage at full tilt. He groaned and clasped his head with one hand, bracing himself from falling to the floor with the other. He tried to sit up but had to lay back down with another groan. His head felt like a giant melon about to split open. He turned his head and tried again to open eyes that were as heavy as sandbags. He couldn't even blink, only try and open the swollen lids a slit.

Total darkness.

Where was he? And who was driving this thing at breakneck speed?

Who they were he couldn't begin to fathom. He could hardly put enough wits together to remember where he had last been, and with whom.

"Thank God, you're rousing," a low, lyrical voice said near him.

He turned toward it instinctively, not remembering if it belonged to someone good or evil. It sounded good.

She sounded good.

Something about it, that soft, low, husky sweetness, touched a deep place that he hadn't remembered since his mother's soft voice had coaxed him from a childhood nightmare. There had been many nightmares, especially when his father was gone from them, Iain watching his kilt flap at the back of his legs as he left for some cause or another. All important missions—stopping tinkers from stealing their sheep and cattle, protecting their lands and fighting with other clans—he understood that much, but still, when he was gone from them the nightmares would return.

"Iain, can you hear me?"

That voice again.

It reached down, drawing something from him; like a bucket in his well, it dipped and demanded something new from him. Something he hadn't ever had to answer to another person to before.

He turned his head away from it.

"Can hear me? MacLeon…Iain?"

Iain turned his head back toward the voice. She sounded afraid.

He tried to sit up and failed, only barely lifting his shoulders. What had they done to him?

"Shhhh," said the gentle voice, and then his head was repositioned, moved onto a soft lap. He resisted the urge to turn into her, to nestle against the warmth and sweet smells of a woman. He turned his head away again, but then she put her hand against his brow. "There now. I can see you need to rest a bit more. I've got you. We're almost there."

Juliet…

He knew her then. Knew her voice and her smell and her softness. He also knew that something terrible had happened to him. Had he been shot? Poisoned? Bludgeoned over the head? He didn't feel pain in any particular area, just an aching head and the knowledge that something was very wrong. And yet he trusted her.

He trusted her like he'd never trusted another breathing soul.

He turned toward her and pressed his nose against her belly. It was there that he trusted her, there that he would know her his whole life.

He took a long breath, pressing into her, and slept again.

~~~~~

"Juliet! Juliet, wake up!"

Juliet woke with a start, the rocking of the carriage having lulled her into a fitful sleep. She looked down at Iain's head still in her lap, slid it to the side onto the seat and rose. She leaned over and turned the latch to the door, opening it a crack.

The earth, still moving beneath them, could be seen and heard beneath the opening of the door. "Ruck! What is it? Are we nearly there?" she yelled it as loud as she could manage up through the crack of the door.

She saw her brother, a long flap of hair over his forehead swinging with the motion of the carriage as he leaned from the coachman's box toward her. "We're close. But it appears we have company."

The minute he said it, a pistol exploded from behind them.

Juliet fell to the floor and pulled the door closed with a scream. On her knees she went to Iain and shook him. "Iain, you must wake. Iain!"

Another shot from a pistol and shouts of men. Oh dear. It had to be Lord Malcolm and his men. They would drag her back to Eden Place, or worse, force her into marriage at Gretna Green with the wrong man. What had they been thinking? They were leading her enemy to a place where they could accomplish their goal so easily.

No. She must stop thinking like that. They couldn't force her to wed. Could they?

Iain was rising to a sitting position, his head in his hands, but his eyes were open. "What've ya done, lass?"

The full weight of what they had done crashed into her, making her grip the seat beside him and look down. How to explain that they had kidnapped him? The MacLeon? It sounded preposterous.

"Tell me quick, lass. I have to know what's to be done."

Juliet nodded. "My brother gave you some laudanum in your drink. I wasn't in agreement with his plan but then, Lord Malcolm...we heard him say that he was going to take me in the morning, this morning, to his home and force me—"

"The two of you carried me to this carriage?" He shook his head and rubbed one hand over his face, still struggling to wake up, it seemed.

"Aye. On a board. 'Tis a long story."

Another pistol shot, closer this time. Iain threw himself on the floor beside her. "And now Malcolm and his men are following us?"

"I believe so. Unless it's highwaymen after us. We are close. Ruck—oh, I'm so worried about Ruck up there on the seat, so exposed! Ruck said we're nearly there."

Iain paused and turned his head toward her, his eyes blazing with intensity. "And just where are we goin', lass?"

Juliet gulped and said in a weak voice, "Gretna Green."

His eyes took on a hint of mirth despite the dire circumstances. "And what did you plan to do once we arrived in Scotland?"

More shouts could be heard and Juliet leaned close to him in fear, her lips trembling as she looked up at him. She could not tell a lie. "Marry." She let that hang there and then rushed out, "It was Ruck's idea but I...I did start to go along with it."

His face went from shocked to hooting out a laugh. "Perhaps you should have taken a more traditional tact and just asked."

Relief pooled through her that he didn't seem to be too angry. Before she had time to think more about that, Iain had pulled a pistol from his belt, scooted across the floor to the door and opened it. "Stay down," he said to Juliet, and then leaned out and around the door, took aim and shot at the men behind them. His arm jerked back as he looked up at Ruck and yelled, "Gretna Green is just over that hill, lad. I'll hold them off, now get those horses moving!"

"MacLeon?" she could hear her brother exclaim. "Thank God, man. I thought you would sleep all day!"

Iain shook his head as he reloaded the pistol with black powder and grinned at Juliet, the crinkles at the sides of his eyes making him look more handsome. "And 'e's complainin' to me." Iain shook his head. "The lad has brass, I'll give him that." He leaned around the door and shot again. Juliet crawled onto the seat and peeked over the back of the seat and out the window. They were too far away to see their faces, but one man had fallen from his horse so it appeared Iain's shots were working—they were falling back.

"I see the village!" Ruck shouted from his high seat.

"None too soon," Iain yelled back. "Head to the blacksmith shop."

"The blacksmith shop? But isn't that where couples go to be married?" Juliet asked, the fact well known.

"Aye." Iain sighed and leaned toward her, his gaze roving across her face and settling on her lips. "'Tis the only way to save you from your fate."

A wild mix of emotion made Juliet's stomach tremble. Was this really what he wanted? "What about your clan? What will they think of a marriage to an Englishwoman?"

"I've less concern of them than what God has arranged."

"God? You mean Ruck?"

He chuckled, grasping her to him in a sudden move that made her squeak. He stared down into her eyes with a look that turned heated, making the breath in her chest pause...waiting...waiting. His head lowered and her eyelids fluttered shut as his mouth closed over hers. This kiss was nothing like that stolen kiss in the garden by the earl. His was branding his own self, his clan, upon her. She could feel it in every fiber of his body straining toward her.

His voice was low and warm in her ear. "Nay, lass, not Ruck. I'm convinced only God's helping hand could have made this plan succeed." He shrugged. "I've been waiting for a sign from Him. I wouldnae have imagined such a harebrained idea as kidnapping the MacLeon but, as I've said, His ways are not my ways."

He seemed so sure. But did she want him marrying her only to save her from Lord Malcolm? Did he love her? He made no mention of the word.

She didn't have time to think it over any further. The carriage came to sudden halt, and as she sat up and looked out the window she saw that they had indeed reached the village and were stopping outside a building with a sign that said "Blacksmith Shop."

Iain took her hand. "We've not much time, lass. We've only scared them off a little. They'll be coming up from behind us at any moment."

Juliet nodded and followed him from the carriage.

They ran toward the door, the three of them, Ruck grinning at Iain's seeming return to health and agreement to the plan.

"He's agreed, then?" Ruck whispered to Juliet as they flung open the wide wooden door.

Juliet nodded, excitement…fear…astonishment…relief—all

expanding from her heart.

"I told you he was in love with you."

"Aye, you did," she said, skirting around him. She laughed as Iain grasped her hand, and she followed him into the large room where the heat of the forging fire made the room bright and warm, reflecting shadow and light on the stone walls.

A large man with a round, florid face turned and greeted them, a dangerous-looking hammer in his hand. "Are ye eager to wed, then?" He took in Iain's tartan, gave a small bow toward him and reached out his hand.

Iain stretched out his arm and clasped the blacksmith's hand in a tight squeeze. "I'm the MacLeon, chief of the Clan MacLeon of the highlands." He turned toward Juliet. "This is Lady Juliet Lindsay of Northumberland and her brother Ruck Lindsay." Iain took a deep breath. "I've not the time to tell the whole tale to you, I fear. A man who thinks he is the better choice of groom will be upon us any minute. We've need of a fast wedding, as fast as may be, my good man."

"Oh, certainly." The blacksmith grinned. "'Tis a specialty of mine, to be sure. Just over here, then." He motioned to a large anvil that sat on a wooden block in the middle of the floor. Nearby was a prayer book, which he picked up and opened to a page that was clearly worn.

"If you would be so kind to repeat after me, MacLeon."

Iain nodded and grasped Juliet's hands in his. They faced each other and in that moment it seemed as if time—all sound and room and persons—dropped away and left only the two of them staring into each other's eyes.

~~~~~~

The blacksmith began to talk in a low and lulling voice the words he was to repeat, but Iain had a hard time concentrating on them—he couldn't take his eyes off his lovely bride's face. Wherefore had this come about? And how was it that he was so blessed happy about it? He'd never imagined, in all his careful ways, an English rose as a bride. Some of her hair—that vibrant red—had come loose from her braid and curled in wisps around her head like an otherworldly halo. The sunlight from the window caught it just so, making it glow around her, and her creamy skin appeared dusted with a rosy flush. Her brown eyes crystallized—like dark diamonds, though he knew not of such a thing. They cut to his heart, a slow and painful thrust that he couldn't resist, making it beat like a beast.

He felt strong beside her, as if his body were now her shield, his efforts now multiplied, bursting with promise—the promise of her, and them together, and the family that would follow. Sons and daughters, pray God—a heart's cry that he'd never acknowledged being fulfilled lay in those dark brown eyes.

"MacLeon?"

He tore his gaze away toward the blacksmith's kind and knowing eyes. "I've not heard a word, I fear."

The blacksmith held the book toward him. "Would you like to read them, then?"

"Aye."

It was a risky question, for many couldn't read, but Iain thought that the blacksmith might have heard of his unusual education at the University in Edinburgh. He took the book with one hand, holding Juliet's hand with the other, and began where the blacksmith pointed.

"I take you to be my wife and I pledge to you the faith of my body, that I will be faithful to you and loyal with my body and my goods and that I will keep you in sickness and in health and in whatever condition it will please the Lord to place you, and that I shall not exchange you for better or worse until the end."

The blacksmith nodded, appreciation glowing from his eyes. He took the book back and said to Juliet, "Would you like to repeat after me?"

"I will read it as well."

Both men paused. It was assumed Juliet could not read. A slow smile grew upon her face as she took the book. She looked at Iain and whispered, "We've much to learn of each other."

"Aye, lass. That we do," Iain said in a voice too husky, but he didn't care. She would be his tonight and forever after that. He couldn't imagine anything he had ever wanted more.

Juliet's chin rose and her soft lips repeated the words: "I take you to be my husband and I pledge to you the faith of my body—"

A sudden sounding of horses' hooves and men shouting caused Juliet to start. Her gaze flew to Iain and then the blacksmith.

"Hurry, lass." Iain nodded his encouragement at her.

She rushed out the rest: "That I will be faithful to

you and loyal with my body and my goods and that I will keep you in sickness and in health and in whatever condition it will please the Lord to place you, and that I shall not exchange you for better or worse until the end."

Ruck had flown to the door and was rolling a large stone and some furniture before it.

"There's a lock." The blacksmith nodded toward him. "Used many times before."

Ruck nodded as the blacksmith took their hands and held them up. "No rings?" he quickly asked Iain.

"Not as yet. It will come later."

"Verra good." He bowed to pray as if nothing was wrong, even though the men outside had gathered around the door and were banging on it, trying to get in.

"Ruck." Ian motioned with his head that he get away from the door in case some fool starting shooting at the latch.

"Oh, aye." Ruck rushed back over toward them, the noise growing louder, the yells more threatening and belligerent. So help him, if they harmed a hair on her head…

He looked at the blacksmith with raised brows.

"Ah, yes." The blacksmith cleared his throat and loudly proclaimed, "What God has joined together let no man put asunder. I pronounce you husband and wife." He banged on the anvil with his hammer several harsh blows, making the announcement ring around the room.

A creaking sound and then a shattering sound and then a musket went off with a loud boom. The blacksmith yelled out and fell to the floor.

God help them. They'd broken through.

Chapter Eight

Iain grasped Juliet and pulled her to the floor, half dragging her around the large anvil that had served as the pedestal for the blacksmith's prayer book. Iain saw the man near him grasping the hammer in one of his hands and a long, wicked-looking knife in the other. "'Tis only a flesh wound," he said, motioning his chin toward a bloody shoulder. "I can fight."

Iain nodded, knowing that as a Scot he would most assuredly have his back against any English lord.

The smoke from the shot was clearing. Iain cocked and aimed his pistol toward Lord Malcolm. *Oh no!* He stopped, his heart dropping to his stomach.

"No!" Juliet choked out, seeing it the same time Iain did. Malcolm was holding Ruck to his chest, his pistol pointed at the young man's head.

"Come out! Stand and drop your weapons or the boy dies!" Lord Malcolm jammed the gun into Ruck's temple.

Juliet let out a cry. Ruck visibly trembled from

head to toe.

Iain closed his eyes for a brief moment, sending up a prayer for help. He slowly stood, taking Juliet's hand, helping her rise and looking over to the blacksmith with a nod to do as he said. He left his pistol on the stone floor.

"Your knives and any other weapons, MacLeon," Malcolm snarled. "Don't test me."

Iain reached inside the part of his tartan that covered his chest and drew out a knife that hung by his belt. Next, he took a dagger from a band around his calf and laid it beside the other weapons. The blacksmith did the same. Taking a step closer to Juliet, he slid a small knife from his back and thrust it toward her, blocking the view of what he did with his side and shoulder. He felt Juliet take it, her hand trembling against his for a second. Malcolm's gaze swung back to the pair, squinting at them as if suspicious.

"Send Lady Lindsay to me and you shall have the brother. I've no need of him."

Juliet took a step toward them but Iain stopped her with his hand. "The marriage is legal, Malcolm. You're too late."

"Ha!" Malcolm sneered, his upper lip curling

against his hallow cheeks. "You haven't had time to consummate it, so it's as good as a piece of parchment burned in the fire.
I…will…have…her." He held out his arm and made a come-hither motion to her with his fingers.

Juliet made a sound of anguish from her throat.

Malcolm lowered his chin and gave her a hard stare with his dark eyes.

"The wedding is legal, my lord, I assure you. Even in English law." The blacksmith took a step forward.

Malcolm swung the pistol from Ruck's temple, pointed it at the blacksmith's head and pulled the trigger faster then any of them could have anticipated. Juliet screamed as the blacksmith fell, a large hole in the middle of his forehead beginning to burst with blood.

Iain's body grew tense and ready to spring at any moment. It was a madman he was dealing with.

"Juliet! Hie yourself over to me immediately!" He had another pistol in his hand, probably from one of his men, who were all pointing weapons at them. There were more of them than Iain had first thought. Twenty or so.

Malcolm grasped Ruck's hair in his hand, making

the young man grunt, and thrust him forward, the pistol at his back. "On the count of three, if you are not beside me, I will shoot your dearest brother." His voice lowered to a silken purr. "But if you come willingly, I will release him and he can go as he pleases to live a life free of debt, and possibly, one day, a friend to us with many connections and advantages. I don't think you've thought this through, my dear. A wild Scottish highlander may seem romantic now, but it would be a life in a frozen hell, in the wilds, working yourself to skin and bones. I...I will give you everything you could ever wish for. Money...power... You will rule every ballroom."

Iain saw a tear, and then two, trickle down Juliet's cheeks. She was shaking her head, a hopeless look of terror on her face.

Malcolm narrowed his eyes at her tears. "*One*," he said in a voice laced with evil.

Juliet let out a wail, her gaze swinging to Iain. Iain shook his head but knew they had no choice. So much pain radiated from his chest that he thought it would burst. He took a deep breath.

"*Two*." The gun at her brother's back pressed harder, making Ruck cry out.

"Don't do it, Juliet." Ruck shook his head but his

eyes were full of fear.

"Th—"

Iain took Juliet's arm and brought her from around him to in front of him, rasping low into her ear as she moved around his side, "Stay alive. I *will* come for you."

~~~~~

Juliet couldn't feel her slipper-shod feet as she tottered toward her brother. She could hear her own whimpering, but felt like they were coming from another. A part of her detached and floated in agony toward the man who would have her at any cost.

When she reached Ruck, she grasped him and held him to her. Malcolm reached around, grasped her upper arm in a tight squeeze that made her cry out and simultaneously pulled her toward his boney chest while pushing her brother toward Iain.

"A wise move, MacLeon, though I was looking forward to killing you." He tilted his head and gave Iain an eerie smile. "Perhaps another time."

~~~~~

"If you harm her in any way…" Iain narrowed his eyes and clenched his empty fists, his fingers tingling, longing for the sure grip of his sword.

Malcolm threw back his head and laughed. "As if you have any say in my affairs. She'll be my wife tonight, MacLeon, not yours. Go to your bed thinking about that." He chuckled dark and deep, motioned to his men with an upraised arm and swung himself and Juliet around, his dark cloak flying out, taking his wife inside of it, taking her with him.

Iain fell to one knee as they fled the room and mounted their horses. He dropped his head into his cupped hands and clenched his eyes closed, breathing deeply, focusing on God's voice, knowing he couldn't do this alone.

After a few breaths he felt a shift inside his spirit—a turning away from the tragedy at hand and a turning toward Him. A peace slowly crept over him—not a good-will sort of peace that took away all feeling, all danger; no, this was a deeply sated calm to the depths of his being but still with a knife's edge of fight—victory humming along its waves in a somehow strange and perfect accord.

He looked up to see Ruck staring down at him as if he'd gone mad, breathing heavily. "Will you pray like an old woman?" he demanded with tears in his eyes. "We have to go after them."

Iain rose and clapped Ruck on one shoulder, his voice and eyes somber. "Aye, we will rescue her."

"How?" Ruck rubbed a hand over his eyes, dashing the tears away. "There's too many of them." His arm swept toward the blacksmith. "He shot him without provocation." His voice trembled and Iain wondered if this was the first man he'd ever seen shot down. "He's capable of anything."

Iain looked at the blacksmith and shook his head. It was as the boy said—Lord Malcolm was without a scrap of honor and would do anything to get what he wanted. They had to take care of the blacksmith first.

"Come then, lad. Let's find the sheriff or whatever law is in this village."

They hurried to the busiest establishment, a pub a few doors down the cobbled road, and were soon directed to a man sitting at one of the tables, Sherriff McKinney.

"'Tis a pity, 'tis a pity, indeed," he kept saying as Iain told of what happened. "Such a good mon, the blacksmith. And takin' your new bride." He shook his head as if was unheard of. "Well." He rubbed his hands together and reached for his hat and musket. "I'll gather the lads and give instructions to Mrs. McCreedy to see to the body. Meet me out front of the blacksmith shop with fresh horses. You ken their direction, do ya now?"

Iain nodded. "I believe he's taking her back to Northumberland, to his home, which is a neighboring estate to the Lindsay lands. About two days' ride if they hurry." Iain didn't let himself think of that final threat, but the fact that they might stop for the night… "They have about an hour's lead."

The sheriff looked him in the eyes with a knowing stare, nodded a little and clapped Iain on the shoulder. "We'll get to them in time, lad. Fear not."

Even though Iain was the head of the clan now, a leader and old enough to not need a father so much, the sudden feeling of fatherly support, of someone comforting *him*, overcame Iain and he felt a load being lifted from his shoulders. "I believe you."

Within another half-hour Iain and Ruck sat mounted on fresh horses and saw what looked like a troop of soldiers come around the bend in the road toward them. Iain's heart thrummed with the sight of them—at least twelve men, and trained. What they were doing in Gretna Green he didn't know, nor overly care. He'd needed a militia and, and praise be to God, he just got one.

~~~~~~

They'd stopped. She couldn't see where, as they'd put a flour sack over her head, but she felt the sudden lack of movement and Lord Malcolm's body sway against her. They'd forced her arms around his body and tied them together at his stomach. She'd fought it at first, not touching him nor leaning upon him, but after the first few miles knew it for a fruitless endeavor. If she were to stay atop this horse, she would have to cling to her captor.

Stay alive. I will come for you.

She repeated the words in her head anytime she felt the least nauseous from the swaying of the horse, the least guilty for grasping hold of her captor, in the moments of terror when she heard their plans for stopping for the night and dread for what was to come.

Iain would come for her. *Her husband* would not forsake her.

"Get her off!" Lord Malcolm barked the order to someone she couldn't see. She felt rough hands grasp her around the waist and pull her toward the ground. She resisted the urge to kick out at him, to fight. She would save that until she really needed it. It would only anger them now.

She felt the man stumble back as he pulled her off and heard a grunt and then her own screech as he pulled her to the ground and on top of him. The scratchy burlap was lifted off her head. She gulped the fresh air, seeing that it was dusk, and rolled off Malcolm's man, awkward in her movements with her hands still bound together.

"We will camp here for the night. Prepare the tents and a small fire. You there, Reginald—untie her hands and see that she attends her needs. Watch her closely." He glared at the man in warning. Juliet looked at the man in charge of her and was somewhat relieved to see a younger man, not much older than Ruck. It was a logical choice, she supposed. He bent to the task of untying her hands, a red flush filling his cheeks, dark hair over his eyes. As soon as her wrists were free she shook them, the feeling of pins and needles making her lean back her head and shut her eyes. "My thanks," she muttered low to the lad.

He couldn't seem to look at her. No wonder, with the ribald comments among the men about what was in store for her with their lord tonight.

Juliet took a breath and spoke low and sure to him. "If you'll just walk with me toward that steam there..."

She could feel Malcolm's eyes on them as she

dusted off her skirts. She did not look at him. She couldn't. Her gaze, instead, scanned the area, seeing green hills on every side and a trickling, gentle stream just ahead. She knew this land. Northern England. They were going toward home—his home.

She washed her face in the stream, picking up the heaviest rocks with one hand and shoving them deep in her skirt pockets. The knife! She'd forgotten Iain had given it to her when Malcolm had demanded that he lay his weapons on the ground. Did she still have it?

With casual movements, still kneeling by the stream, she reached into her other pocket. Yes, there it was. She took a deep breath and imagined having to use it. She swallowed hard, thinking of the blood and not knowing…where did one thrust it? She clamped her teeth together in determination. She would know. She would be so desperate that she would know.

She looked up into the shadows of a grove of trees, stood and said to the young man, "I'll be but a minute."

As she neared it, another thought came to her. Dare she? It was growing dark. She had a weapon.

Dare she try and escape?

Chapter Nine

The men spread out around the dark campsite, a soft rustling of movement against the chirrup of insects and whisper of flying geese overhead. Iain looked up at the starry sky and took a long breath of the frosty autumn air. *Thank thee, Lord, for thy help. Please now that we should overcome our enemies.*

He looked down the sloping valley at the campsite where Malcolm had stopped for the night. There was a campfire being attended to by one of Malcolm's men, small tents surrounding it. The horses were hobbled to the left under an overcropping of hillside and near a stand of trees. It was a logical place to keep them, out of the elements, but it also made for an easy hiding place for someone to loosen their lines. He nodded, his gaze scanning the area for a woman, for his woman.

His wife.

That he was wed had not really sunk in. Not that he'd had time to consider all that had happened in the last two days. God willing, in a few days he would be bringing home a wife, an English wife to present to his clan and his mother. Matilda MacLeon was a kind and wise woman, but Iain's throat still tightened thinking of presenting a stranger to her. Juliet would need her support to have any chance of gaining the clan's approval, but he didn't know... they would have expected a proper wedding with all in attendance.

A sudden clamoring came from below. Iain sank farther behind the rock he was hiding behind along with the other men in their troop, watching, gauging the danger. Iain squinted in the darkness as two men came from the far side of the fire, a woman, struggling and screeching, between them. His heart dropped to his stomach. It was Juliet. If he strained he could make out some of what was said.

Malcolm came out, an angry march, with his cape flaring out. "What is the meaning of this!"

"She tried to escape, my lord. We chased her down, though, didn't we, Reggie?"

A slight young man stuttered his agreement. "We got her, my lord."

"You did, did you?" Malcolm reached out and hit the boy across the side of his head with his fist. He went down like he'd been shot. "Fools, the lot of you. She's a mere skirt and look at you, breathing heavy like aged men." The other man released Juliet and backed away before Malcolm could strike him. Juliet stood still now, looking at Malcolm, her face in the firelight determined, her gaze not flinching, remaining on her captor.

Malcolm seemed to enjoy her courage, because he chuckled and took her chin in a tight grip. His voice lowered so that Iain couldn't make it out, but he saw her face pale while shaking her head no. It was a good thing he hadn't heard it; it was all he could do to not march toward the man right this instant and put a shot through his head. Iain took a long breath, realizing that he had been practically standing while watching the scene. Malcolm grasped her by the arm and jerked her toward him, walking her toward the largest tent.

Iain crept over to the sheriff. "We can't wait. He means to...*take her* now."

The sheriff nodded. "Aye. But we can't charge just yet. Hold yourself, MacLeon. 'Tis difficult, I ken. But we must for a little bit yet, you see?"

Iain did see, the logical side of him did, but the other side, the side that had vowed to protect her over his own life, wasn't going to wait long.

"I say we create a distraction. Those horses." Iain

pointed to the stand of trees. "We could quickly get two or three men to release them, drive them into the camp, and then they could scurry up those hills to a hiding spot. Several other men can move in close, surround the camp to cover them. I'll head down, as close as I can get to Malcolm's tent, and wait. As soon as he leaves the tent to see what is happening, I will take Juliet where we left Ruck and then come back and join the fight."

The sheriff nodded, looking at his feet. "'Tis a good plan." He looked back up at Iain, and Iain saw a steely determination light his eyes. "I want Malcolm alive, if God be willin'. He's to hang for what he did to Henry."

"The blacksmith?"

"Aye, 'is given name, it was."

Iain clapped him on the shoulder. "You shall have him."

~~~~~

Fire ripped through Juliet's shoulder as Lord Malcolm jerked her inside his tent. Once inside, he flung her away from him so hard that she fell to the ground on a mound of furs that was to be their bed. Light flickered from a lantern, casting eerie shadows of the man who was her captor. He moved like an angry predator, back and forth and back and forth, a wavering shadow that loomed above her.

"You thought to escape, did you?" His voice was low and rasping, a dark mirth underlying his words. "You thought you could outwit me?" He stopped pacing suddenly, turning toward her as a sudden change came over him. There was such rage on his face that her breath froze in her throat. A little sound, a sound so pathetic and terrified, came from her throat.

Oh, God. Please, help me.

He glared down into her face, inches away. "You thought to outwit me!" he whisper-yelled, spittle coming from his lips. He got even closer and grasped her chin hard, shaking her head. "You little beggar. You don't know who you are dealing with yet, do you?" He moved closer, his breathing heavy and harsh, and then he pressed his mouth to hers.

Juliet screamed against the pressure on her lips and pushed at his shoulders as they crashed into her. She fell back with a sob, his hands going toward her breasts. Panic overwhelmed her—hands clawing, feet kicking, jerking her head away. He reached up and grabbed hold of her hair with one hand, the other pressing harder and harder into the soft flesh of her breast.

Stay alive

The words came fast and sudden into her consciousness. She wasn't doing this right. He expected—wanted, even—a fight.

I will come for you

Iain was coming. She had to buy time. She had to distract him. She had to play…his…game.

She went limp and compliant. Took a shattering breath and turned her face toward his.

He paused. Reared back and looked at her with suspicion.

"Wait, my lord," she begged. "Perhaps…." She looked away as if embarrassed, allowing the flush to come up her chest and neck and into her face. "Perhaps you are right." She turned and looked him in the eye. She made herself believe the next words. There would be no second chance at this scheme. She had to make him believe her.

A tear trickled from one eye and slid down her temple into her hair. "I think…" She paused a moment, as if the words were hard to admit, her chest panting. "…you may have been correct in your assessment at the blacksmith's shop."

"Yes?" His eyes grew intrigued but still guarded, very guarded. She had to play on his weakness—his pride.

"I think perhaps I may have not have thought things through and have acted rashly, my lord. Your arguments…" She looked down in mock modesty and whispered, "The things you said about our wealth and power at court as a couple…I had not considered such a life at any length but now I believe. I…I, pray forgive me, am young and impulsive and you were rather distant when we first met. I let a fool's romantic thoughts of the highlands carry me away." She let a slow smile slide across her face and looked up at him. "I didn't realize you had such strength, such passion, my lord. Perhaps we are well suited after all."

He was fighting it, she could tell by the tightness in his lips and the tremor in his arms braced on either side of her, but he backed away, sat on his heels and studied her as if to judge her words. And his eyes were pleased.

She was almost there.

She cleared her throat. "Might we have something to drink? I should like to get to know you better." She forced admiration into her gaze.

He wavered, tilting his head and studying her

intently.

Her heartbeat was so loud in her ears that she feared he could hear it and detect her game. She forced a small, encouraging smile, a look of promise filling her gaze. She didn't know exactly how she knew how to give those kinds of looks, but it was something she had always had, something that had always attracted men to her—her voice, which she lowered automatically to suit the web she was spinning, and now these looks, heated and purposeful but with a degree of challenge and patience, like a cat eyeing its prey.

He turned and reached for the wine cask. While his back was to her she let out a silent breath of relief and sat up. Now to get him talking. He enjoyed talking about himself, didn't he? He must.

"Tell me of your home, my lord. I know it is close to Eden Place but I've never seen it."

"It's three times the size of Eden, which, by the way, is ours, you know." He held out a cup with deep red wine.

"Ours?" She felt genuine surprise. "How can that be?" Ruck was the eldest son and should inherit any estate her father had left behind.

He tilted his head in that strange way as his lips

curved up in a joker's smile. "When I paid off your father's debts I bought it. It was part of our agreement, you and Eden. Your family is free to live there, provided you mean what you say." His voice turned deadly.

Juliet changed the topic, not able to think about her family right now. "And your home. Are you there often or do you also enjoy a townhome in London? You mentioned balls. Do you enjoy the season, my lord?"

He chuckled and a deep shiver went down her spine that she tried to disguise by turning onto her right hip on the furs. "I have little use for balls or soirees. Parliament, though…I am"—his narrow chest puffed out—"one of the most influential members of Parliament."

Juliet smiled. "I couldn't doubt it."

He turned toward her, a quirk in his brow. "Couldn't you?" He smirked. "You were trying to run off not an hour ago."

She bit down on her tongue. She mustn't overplay this hand. She looked down, averting her eyes. "I was afraid." Her voice was low and deep.

"Afraid of me?" He sounded offended by it.

"My lord, you forget I am only twenty and not

used to such...powerful figures as yourself." She thought quickly of Iain and hurried on. "The MacLeon was more my brother's idea than mine, and the Scotsman didn't even wake from the laudanum Ruck gave him until we were nearly at the church."

"I don't believe it!" He said the words but sounded pleased at the same time, as if he did believe it.

Emboldened, Juliet looked up and nodded. "It's true. We panicked, Ruck and I, not knowing you. Pray forgive us. Let us start anew."

"Anew?" His eyes took on a confused and yet intrigued light.

Juliet nodded. "A church wedding, as is proper. As you know, nothing has happened between the MacLeon and I. I'd have our lives start out as the church commands: blessed by the church, for our future and our future children." She glanced down at the furs and said low, with conviction, "Not with violence to be punished by God."

There. She had used an argument that he could not contend against. Like any good Catholic, Lord Malcolm might only fear one thing—the church and its laws and superstitions. She had come as close as she could to saying that if he forced her, God might punish him with a life without an heir.

She looked up to see him sipping his wine and giving her that long and uncomfortable stare.

Suddenly he threw back his head and roared with laughter. With one giant gulp he drained his cup and threw it aside. As if time were suspended, she watched the cup roll through the grass, her heartbeat speeding and speeding and roaring in her ears, like a pot coming to full boil and then boiling over.

Dear God, she'd failed.

The knowledge slammed into her as fast as he did. He rose onto his knees and lunged toward her, too quick for her to move.

She screamed as he fell on her. "Nice try, my pretty little conniving wench." He grasped her hair and forced her head up toward his. Her gaze locked on his crazed one. She screamed again but not very loud as her throat was frozen in terror.

Chapter Ten

Iain heard the scream and knew he couldn't wait a second longer. He was crouched just outside the tent and knew his wife was in there with Malcolm. Where were those men with the distraction? He was going to have to go in alone and risk the plan coming apart at the seams.

Just as he rose from his squatted position, the sounds of horses whinnying and loud snorting sounded into the quiet of the night. He looked up and saw the shadow of one of their men untying a lead and pushing the horse toward the campsite. Thank God, it was beginning.

He looked expectantly at the tent where Malcolm held his wife, but the man wasn't coming out to investigate. Other men in the camp were beginning to note the problem, however, and rousing themselves. A sudden shout went up and then several other men rushed to the center of the camp. Pistols and muskets were being loaded, but still no one seemed to be overly panicking.

He was going to have to do something…now.

Raising his pistol, he aimed toward the farthest wooden pole that held up the tent. It was dark and he was breathing heavily but he had to hit the pole; there was no room for error. He squinted down the sight on the barrel and pulled the trigger.

Smoke choked from the pistol, making it impossible to see if he'd hit it for a second or two, and then he heard a snap, a flapping of the tent side collapsing and a bellow of rage from inside the tent.

Malcolm came rushing from the entrance, one hand holding his neck, blood rushing from it. Had Juliet done that? He remembered the knife and grinned.

Malcolm started roaring demands. Iain could just make out the fact that his pants were unbuttoned. His stomach rolled. He was going to be sick…or worse, strangle the man in cold blood.

I want him alive, the sheriff had said. It was the only thing keeping Iain from leaping out and attacking him that very instant.

Stick to the plan.

The words roared inside his head, but his body strained to leave the cover of the brush and rush to his bride.

He watched with held breath as Malcolm marched toward the commotion of the stamping, running horses and his men, spinning around, looking for the cause in the darkness. As soon as Malcolm reached the campfire, Iain took a deep breath, the first in minutes, and pushed gently out of the brush to pad across the short distance of grass to the tent's entrance.

He pushed back the flap and rushed inside. "Juliet?" The tent was dark and half fallen in. He heard a sob and then felt her press into his arms. She was trembling from head to toe and held a bloody knife in her hand.

He squeezed her tight to him and whispered, "You stabbed him?"

She nodded against his chest, a sob escaping.

"Shhhh, it's all right now. Let's go." He took the knife from her, wiped it in the grass, shoved it in his belt and took her hand. He opened the tent flap a little and peered out, listening. The commotion had been joined by the musket shots. "Stay down," he instructed Juliet.

Crouching, they crept from the tent back toward the hiding place where Iain had been. Once behind the thick cover of branches, they stopped for breath. Iain turned to assess the situation. Malcolm was leading his men toward the hill and stream, looking for the sheriff's men. Out of the corner of his eye Iain saw a dash of white and realized that Malcolm had sent one of his men back to the tent to guard Juliet. He motioned for Juliet to get farther down as the man ran into the tent and then out again. He would rush to tell Malcolm, and Iain couldn't let that happen.

Leaning across the top of one dense bush, he pulled his pistol forth and stretched it toward the man. A sound of a blast came from their right side before he could take aim. The man fell to the ground. Darting around, Iain saw the sheriff perched on a small cliff just across on their right side. With a wave the sheriff let Iain know that he had been watching and that he knew Juliet was with him. He'd been covering them all along. Iain took a deep breath of relief and sank down next to his bride.

"Juliet, listen carefully." He gently took her face into his hands and turned it toward him. Her eyes were wide with shock and full of tears. "Shhhh, my sweet, 'tis going to be all right, you know."

She shook her head. "What do we do? There are so many of them."

"I'm here with the sheriff from Gretna Green and a dozen militia. We can win this fight." He squeezed her shoulder and pointed downhill, away from the camp, where they had first ridden in. "See that stream? We're going to follow it back toward the road to Gretna Green. About two leagues is our camp; it's hidden in the hallows of those foothills.

"You can't send me there alone." She clutched his arm with a desperation he'd never seen in her. Had Malcolm succeeded before she stabbed him? Just the thought made him want to retch, but now was not the time to ask.

"Nay, lass. I will take you there."

He took her hand and pulled her behind him down into the valley along the stream, shots still ringing out behind them.

Dark, shadowy clouds moved with the wind, the moonlight coming and going, glistening over the stream as they rushed, their breath thick and heavy in the still night, away from the scene. As soon as they were far enough away to no longer hear the blasts of shots, Iain pulled Juliet to the side, to a large, flat stone and bade her sit down and catch her breath.

"But should we stop?" She was holding her side and he knew she had a stitch there.

"Just for a moment."

She gulped air and nodded. When she'd caught her breath enough to talk, she rushed out all the questions she must have been thinking. "What's to happen? Did the blacksmith survive? I feel so horrible." She looked up at him with pain-stricken eyes, her skin luminous in the sharp light. "He's dead, isn't he?"

"Aye." Iain looked briefly away and wiped a hand over his eyes, feeling suddenly tired. "The sheriff and the militia came to our aid because of the blacksmith's death. They mean to see Lord Malcolm hang for it, though I don't know that they have the power to hold him here in Scotland."

"So it's the blacksmith's death that could save us." She shook her head, tears in her eyes. "It's not fair. I just... Ruck and I... Is Ruck with them?"

Iain squatted down in front of her and took her hand. "We ordered him to stay behind at the camp and hold it against any that might come by and discover us. He wasnae too happy about it, I can tell you. But if he's obeyed me, then he is safe."

"Pray God he listened."

"Are you rested, then?" Iain pulled her up and into his arms, looking down into her face, her hair a disarray of long, dark tresses around her shoulders.

"Aye." She'd taken his way of saying "yes."

He wanted to ask what had happened with Malcolm, could hardly stop the questions from escaping his lips, but if she told him something he couldn't bear, he didn't think he would be able to stick with the plan. He would send her back to their camp alone and turn back, go and slit the throat of Lord Malcolm. He shuddered with the thought of it.

"MacLeon!" A whispered shout stopped him. He turned and reached for his pistol and then shoved Juliet behind him. They both turned toward the voice.

"Don't shoot, for goodness' sake!" Her brother came from behind a thick tree with his hands up. "It's just me."

"Ruck!" Juliet pushed away from Iain with a desperate sound coming from her throat and ran to her brother, throwing her arms around him and nearly knocking him to the ground.

Iain ran after her. What was the lad doing so far from their camp?

He answered Iain's unspoken question as soon as Iain was upon them. "There was no one around for so long I determined the camp didn't need minded after all."

"Orders are not to be disobeyed, nor determined by your own judgment of the situation," Iain said, his gaze sweeping the horizon for danger.

Ruck nodded and shrugged. "I suppose so, but I thought you might need me."

He seemed so genuine, so young and eager, that Iain didn't have the heart to upbraid him more. *Dear Lord, is this what it is going to be like? Having a younger brother?* He found there was already a special place carved out in his heart for the lad. A protective place, a fatherly place, a place that would grow and later also be there for his sons.

"I do need you," Iain stated in a grave voice. He pulled out the knife that he had given to Juliet and handed it over to Ruck, hilt side out. "Take your sister back to the camp and hide her." When Ruck started to protest, Iain took a step toward him and looked down at him with all the seriousness he had. "I would trust no one aside from myself the task. 'Tis as dangerous a mission as mine. They came for one thing and will want one thing if they overcome us. Juliet."

Ruck's face took on the gravity of the situation. "Do you fear defeat?"

"Nay, never fear it. Plan for it, aye. If we do not return..." He turned to Juliet and promised with deep conviction, "I will return." To Ruck he finished, "If we do not return you must take Juliet to my home in the highlands. You must tell them what happened. They will protect you."

"But how will I know the way?" Ruck asked.

Iain took strip of leather from his belt, where it hung ready to tie something to it. Next, he took a heavy gold ring from his finger, strung it onto the lace and tied the ends together. He turned toward Juliet and placed it around her neck, slipping the ring inside her bodice where it couldn't be seen. "The MacLeon seal is engraved on the ring. It will keep you safe in Scotland and provide guidance."

"But Iain..." Juliet reached toward him.

He took her by the shoulders and brought her close, looking down into her lovely brown eyes. "I told you I would come for you and I came for you. I tell you now I will be return. Faith...not fear, wife."

He felt her stand straighter as an inner resolve struck her backbone. She nodded and reached up on tiptoes to kiss him. Out of the corner of his eye he saw that Ruck had turned away, which made him smile as he leaned down and kissed her back.

His mouth moved over hers, tasting her, remembering her soft lips.

It was their first kiss as husband and wife and he vowed it wouldn't be the last.

Chapter Eleven

Juliet reminded herself several times over the next hour to have faith. She realized, sitting in the dark next to her brother, sheltered by an outcropping of moss-covered rock, that there might be many times in the coming years when Iain would have to leave for battle. Her father had never had to do such a thing that she could remember, so it wasn't something she had watched her mother endure. She looked over at Ruck and knew that he too might have to go and fight for king and country some day. He was almost of an age to join a British militia, and he looked eager for it. It was the duty of the women to stay behind, keep the household running and hope and pray for their men to return alive. For her there would be a clan of other women and children left behind to keep at peace, to reassure, to comfort when things went wrong. As she looked ahead toward her future she saw that she was going to be a leader, whether she liked it or not.

Time to start acting like one.

She stood up and felt for the knife. "Ruck, what

weapons have you?"

Ruck stood, a puzzled frown on his face. "This pistol and a knife. Why? Juliet, what are you thinking?"

"I'm thinking we have been hiding long enough. I'll not put us in any unnecessary danger, but we have to go back and see what is happening. They are outnumbered and they may need us."

"MacLeon will have my head if I let you do this." Ruck dug in his heels, scowling.

"We won't be fighting with Iain, just assessing the situation."

"Well, all right." The gleam of adventure had come into his eyes and Juliet knew he couldn't help but be excited to see what action might be occurring.

They hurried back to the campsite, the cold light of the moon helping them see the path. As they neared, they spotted a good place where they could look down and see without being seen, and crouched down behind the tall brush.

"It's so quiet," Ruck commented.

Indeed it was, deathly so. Juliet made a motion with her hand and crept even closer to the next group of bushes. She peeked around the edge of the brush, seeing a small, dying fire and the tents, some fallen, glowing under the eerie light. There were three bodies on the ground. Juliet's pulse raced in her ears as she searched for Iain.

A scream suddenly split through the air.

Juliet stiffened, every nerve humming with shock. "Look!" She pointed to several dark, moving forms across the way, back up on the hillside where the road toward home lay. "Come on."

Ruck was already on his feet in a hunched position and moving closer. Juliet picked up her skirts and kept pace with him. They got close enough where they could start to make out voices.

"Let us go and she lives."

Juliet strained to see. There was Iain; she knew his form instantly. He was standing with several men on one side while Lord Malcolm and his men were on the other side. She blinked, wondering if her eyes were playing tricks on her as she stared at Lord Malcolm. He was holding a woman against his chest, just as he had with Ruck at the blacksmith's shop. The woman turned her head and Juliet almost moaned aloud. Her heart dropped.

"It's Mother." Ruck gasped. "What is she doing here?"

Juliet didn't know, but it couldn't be good.

"Come now, Lord Malcolm," one of the men on Iain's side was saying, his gun pointed toward the pair of them, "you'll not want another murder on your hands, now, will ya?"

"Self-defense. Any law in the land of England will back me against a Scottish tradesman," Lord Malcolm sneered.

"Aye, perhaps, but against a lady? Your own betrothed's mother? I ken that would be another story."

"Shut up." He looked at Iain. "I've gotten what I wanted from Juliet, and no longer have any use for her. She isn't the alliance I require. If you repay the debt I paid for Lord Lindsay and the cost of Eden you may have her, damaged goods that she is, free and clear. You've killed five of my men; let us end this and go unmolested."

Juliet clenched her jaw, anger filling her at what Lord Malcolm insinuated. He was playing some dark game. She hoped Iain wouldn't fall for any tricks.

"And their mother? She can return home

unharmed?" Iain's deep, calm voice made Juliet's breath ease. He had a plan. He knew what he was doing. *Have faith. Have faith.*

"I will drop her off on my way. You have my word," Lord Malcolm stated.

Her mother twisted against him. "He lies! It's burned to the ground. Everything! There is no more Eden—"

Lord Malcolm cut off her words by choking her with his arm.

Ruck started to get up, but Juliet pulled him back. "Wait," she whispered.

"We have to save her!" Ruck's face was chiseled with misery in the strange light.

"Wait." Juliet nodded to him, silently reminding him to have faith as well.

"Leave her with us and you may go," Iain stated with authority, holding out his hand toward their mother. "Now."

Lord Malcolm hesitated and then pushed Lady Lindsay over toward him. She gasped for air but rushed to his side. Iain pushed her behind him, his pistol and the pistols of the sheriff and his men pointing at Lord Malcolm's men as they turned and mounted the few horses they must have been able to round up. She watched in disbelief as they turned their horses to leave. Was he really going to get away with murdering the blacksmith? Would he really leave them alone if Iain paid off the debt? She doubted it.

Juliet had started to rise when a shot rang out.

Ruck pulled her back behind the bush, but not before she saw Lord Malcolm slump in his saddle and slide off his horse to the ground.

~~~~~~

Iain looked around and saw the sheriff standing with his legs braced apart, a smoking pistol in his hands. He looked over at Iain and winked. "Self-defense."

Iain gaze snapped to Malcolm's men, expecting returning fire, but saw that they were galloping away, obviously not concerned about the state of their master.

He stood there in some shock at the turn of events. The sheriff clapped him on the shoulder. "I'm thanking the good Laird for the moonlight this eventide." He grinned. "I'd nae have gotten the shot without it."

Iain shook his head. "It would have been better to

go to trial...see justice done."

"Aye, it would 'ave. But the man was right. He would 'ave gotten off had it even seen a trial. The law favors the rich and the nobles. 'Tis a shame, but 'tis the way o' things."

Iain took a long breath, agreeing.

"We'll see to the body. You go and fetch your bride." He stopped and turned his head suddenly toward Iain. "Why, you haven't even made it official yet, have you, MacLeon?"

Juliet was thankful for the shadows that concealed the rush of warmth that filled her face.

"Gretna Hall, that's where you'll take her. Her ladyship and Lord Ruck can stay with my wife and me for a few days until you decide what to do."

"'Tis kind of you," Iain acknowledged.

Lady Lindsay huffed. "I'll not be staying with strangers. Where is my son?"

"Here!" Ruck stood up suddenly and waved, yelling. He started up the hill toward them. With a little sound, Juliet hurried after him.

Iain met her halfway and took her into his arms. "What are you doing here?" He looked pleased and angry at the same time. "I told you to stay with

Ruck."

"Ruck is here."

"'Tis not what I meant." He looked as if he was deciding to kiss her or strangle her. She decided to make the choice for him, reaching up and wrapping her arms around his neck. "I know. I'm sorry. I-I had to see if you were okay." Her lips parted as she moved closer.

His lips crashed down over hers, taking his frustration into the devouring movement of his mouth against her mouth. Juliet's senses spun, making her lightheaded and breathless. She forgot where they were, who might be watching— everything except the man that was her husband.

He broke away, his breathing ragged. "You'll not disobey again?"

"Not today," she promised with breathless sincerity, grinning up at him.

He broke into a loud laugh. "You'll be the death of me, lass."

"Nay." She shook her head, her eyes brimming with happiness. "I'll be the life of you."

His eyes turned soft and filled with love. "Aye. That you will, wife. That you will."

Epilogue

Eilean Donan Castle, Christmas Day

A fortnight of travel.

After a fortnight of helping her mother and Ruck clean up the devastation of Eden Place and see to the beginnings of their new home, Iain sending letters and notes of credit and stretching their coin as far as it would go. Sheep. That was what he kept saying. They needed more sheep. Everywhere, sheep! And Ruck was Iain's shadow, gleaning everything from her husband that he could and preparing to be the man of the house and set up his sheep farm and new house. Her mother had become surprisingly acquiescent to them all. She seemed happy for the first time that Juliet could remember; she and Claire planning some fittings and furnishings for the new house, all the while staying without complaint in the gardener's house, who had gladly moved in with a friend so that the young lord and ladies of the house would have somewhere to lay their heads while the construction took place. They should be in the first part of the house within a month—not too long to endure a stone cottage.

Juliet smiled, so tired on her mount that she was a bit silly-happy, thinking of the first time she saw Iain with a sheep. Goodness, he loved them. One would think they were gold bars—which they were, according to her husband.

Husband.

Three fortnights of marriage. Fortnights of discovery and hidden moments between the exhaustion of all the tasks they had before them. She took a sudden inhale, thinking of their tangled covers, his strong back under her hands…exploring, his hands…exploring…those long, deep kisses…

Fie! She mustn't think such thoughts in the daylight. She looked away and took another long breath and then looked over at him, just ahead of her on his horse.

As if he felt her gaze, he turned and looked at her, snatching her breath again, the sun shining just so on his hair, making it alive with light, his eyes merry and eager. They were almost there. To Eilean Donan, his castle, his clan, his life.

"The bridge! Do you see it?" He pointed, and Juliet peered through the mist to see a long stone bridge, arches underneath reaching deep into the water. Eilean Donan sat on an island where three great lochs met—Loch Long, Lock Duich and Lock Alsh. Surrounded by wood and braced by the steep inclines of hills covered in every shade of green, it was as she had ridden into a fairy place, a place that was more heaven than earth. Even more beautiful than where she'd first met this man, her husband, Iain MacLeon, with her cousin in Glencoe. This was Glencoe with lochs and a castle and mist that undulated across the middle of the mountains like a sash of smoke.

Iain had slowed to match her horse's stride. "Do you like it?"

Her throat was so tight she couldn't yet speak, so she only nodded and held back tears.

They came around a small bend and she saw the castle in the distance. Made of dark stone and massive against the mountain, it took up the landscape like a giant refuge. A fortification for the nearby villages in times of trouble and a guardian of the lochs, standing firm against any who might come to invade the land that was Scotland.

"You don't like it." His voice was dry.

She looked over at him with tears in her eyes.

"Nay, I love it. It's just that...I'm afraid."

"Afraid?" He tilted his chin toward her. "What's to be afraid of, wife?"

"It's all so grand." She shook her head, unable to explain it. "The land, your land, it makes me want to weep, 'tis so beautiful." She dashed away the tears, embarrassed.

"Aye! It makes me want to weep, so thin is the soil. 'Tis why we'll have sheep." He grinned at her and she laughed. The sheep again!

"Will your mother accept me?" It was the question in the darkest, deepest part of her heart...and it felt better to get it into the light.

Iain nodded, his eyes serious. "I've sent word ahead so it shouldnae be a shock. They've had time to get used to the idea." He reached out and grasped for her hand, giving her an intense look. "It may take a bit...but once they know you, they will love what I love."

She nodded, deciding to believe him.

It was a new skill, this faith—trust in a husband and putting faith into what he said and believed. But it felt strong inside her and somehow she knew, instinctively and deep in her being, that together their faith could be impenetrable, not in harsh and overbearing way, never that, in a strong and compassionate way. There may be fiery darts ahead, but together they could conquer anything that was to come.

The horses clattered over the stone bridge and her heart began a drumming march, a singing inside her as the dusk settled around them, the last day of their long journey home.

A sound reached them. A long blast of a horn. And then, the sound of bagpipes and fiddle and fife filled the air. They came to the castle gate, decorated with holly and red ribbon. A man yelled out, "The chieftain of the Clan MacLeon has returned!"

There were cheers coming from everywhere. Juliet looked up and saw rows of people on parapets, on stone stairs, on the lawn of the island that sat at the glistening lochs' convergence. Everywhere was holly and red ribbon and boughs of evergreen—all decked out for Christmas like nothing she'd ever seen.

"And his bride!" the man with the bellowing voice continued. "The Lady MacLeon...Juliet!"

The cheers were just as strong, stronger even, as they resounded against the stone and hillside and mountain and deep of the water in the dusk. Tears rushed down her cheeks. She turned to her husband and asked with trembling joy, "What have you written them?"

Iain dismounted, came to her and pulled her from her horse and into his arms.

He held her close and whispered into her hair. "Only our story. Merry Christmas, my love."

~~~~~~

They'd made it.

They'd made it home by Christmas Day, just as he'd promised in the letter to his mother and the letter to his clan. He hadn't lied to Juliet—he had written them of their story and all that had happened…well, nearly all. And he'd reminded them of the power of love—of human love and God's love and the love of a Father who sent a Son to save them on Christmas Day. He'd done his best to turn their thoughts away from their differences—the English and the Scottish—and turn them toward what they shared: love of the highlands, love of a man or woman, love of God. And then he'd prayed that they would give Juliet a chance.

And they had.

He knew the night to come would be filled with

joy and feasting and laughter. And then he would take his bride to the chieftain's bed and show her the full ardor of his love. And then…then they would find their future together.

He took a long, deep breath, joy overflowing, and took Juliet's hand, seeing that she had dried her tears, her chin was raised and her face glowed with the gladness of her destiny upon it.

They began walking through the open gates to his castle—their castle—in the fierce beauty of the Scottish highlands to the thunderous welcome of their people.

Made in the USA
Coppell, TX
27 June 2023